Praise for
Richard S. Wheeler

"Wheeler is a genius."
—*El Paso Herald-Post*

"A modern master of the historical novel."
—*Rocky Mountain News*

"Wheeler is among
the two or three top living writers of
western historicals—if not the best."
—*Kirkus Reviews*

"Wheeler writes characters who never react
or behave like clichés."
—*Booklist*

"A master storyteller whose heart is
obviously in the West."
—*Library Journal*

By Richard S. Wheeler
Published by The Ballantine Publishing Group:

WINTER GRASS
SAM HOOK
STOP
RICHARD LAMB
DODGING RED CLOUD
INCIDENT AT FORT KEOGH
THE FINAL TALLY
DEUCES AND LADIES WILD
THE FATE

INCIDENT AT FORT KEOGH

Richard S. Wheeler

BALLANTINE BOOKS • NEW YORK

A Ballantine Book
Published by The Ballantine Publishing Group
Copyright © 1990 by Richard S. Wheeler

www.randomhouse.com/BB/

ISBN 0-345-44048-X

Manufactured in the United States of America

First Ballantine Books Edition: March 2000

10 9 8 7 6 5 4 3 2 1

For Roger and Nancy Rathke

Prologue

The Legend of Santiago Toole

Many strange and unique people inhabited the American frontier, and among them was Santiago Toole. When he arrived in Milestown, Montana Territory, folks knew he was Irish and a medical doctor, but they couldn't imagine what had brought him—or driven him—from the Emerald Isle to the barren prairies of the American West. Rumor had it that he was the youngest son of an Irish baron, but no one knew how the rumor started. Perhaps it came from Toole himself. But they believed it. His manners, his education, his ways, all spoke of a well-bred man.

A remittance man, they supposed. The West had seen its share of those strange foreigners, paid regular sums by their families to stay away—far away—from home. Toole had to be one of those, living on remittances. Some remittance men were simply wastrels and scoundrels, embarrassments to their respectable parents and grandparents and brothers and sisters. But other remittance men were younger sons of nobles, condemned by the laws of primogeniture never to inherit the great and noble estates of England and Ireland. These younger brothers were a source of constant trouble and bickering, and a drain on the estates, and thus were banished to India, or given an officer's commission in the Royal Army and sent abroad to serve the Empire, or shuffled off to the American frontier. If Toole was really a younger son, it fit. The baron or the inheriting older brother had packed him off to the American West, an ocean and a continent away.

They had it almost right, those shrewd observers of the mannered Irishman who'd settled so improbably in their midst, in rude Milestown hard beside Fort Keogh. Santiago's clever

1

and eccentric father, the baron, christened his youngest son with a Spanish name and provided him with a useful profession. The family would not have the burden of supporting the last of six brothers. Then he packed him off on a White Star steamer, with a medical degree but no remittance at all, and a gentle warning never to set foot in sweet green Ireland again. And never dream of the colleens he'd loved—and forever lost.

And so the young medical doctor had settled in the West, grimly choosing the most brown and bleak place he could find, because anything greener might remind him of the emerald valley of his birth. The Irishman in the black britches and waistcoat and boiled white shirt had built a white clapboard cottage, hung out his shingle, and begun a small practice patching up cowboys and wolfers, sergeants, bawds, elderly mountain men, Cheyenne and Cree and Assiniboin, and breeds of all description.

That's how he met his Mimi, the olive-skinned French-Assiniboin maiden who was carried to him at the brink of death from a strange enteric fever. He'd loved her the moment he saw her flushed face, and when he'd finally restored her to health they remained together. She'd never met a man like Santiago and adored him as much as he loved her. He'd found that she, a breed, was no more accepted by rough frontiersmen than he, a mannered Irishman, but they'd gotten along, eking out a couple hundred dollars a year, mostly paid in beef and horse flesh, chickens and eggs, out of rowdy Milestown.

But as the months passed the rough citizens of that tawdry camp came to appreciate their peculiar doctor. For one thing, this man who could speak the Queen's English so properly could also flatten them with pugilistic tricks they'd never heard of. How could it be? One after another cowboy or soldier would goad the slender physician with the perfect manners into a brawl, and find himself gasping on the ground, winded, staring up into Toole's faint smile.

And that's why, when the sheriff of Custer County resigned and the town fathers couldn't find a proper replacement, they turned to Santiago Toole. Temporarily, of course. No medical doctor, son of an Irish baron, could possibly be much of a frontier sheriff, or do the hard things that all sheriffs do. . . .

But Santiago Toole surprised them again.

Chapter 1

A thunder on the door.

At five in the morning that meant that the caller wanted either the sheriff or the doctor. Santiago Toole was both. A temporary arrangement, of course, until they could hire a proper sheriff to keep the lid on rowdy Milestown, Montana Territory.

He sprang lithely from bed and the warm lean form of his French-Assiniboin lady Mimi. She stirred, and reached out to him, and the sleep-swept gesture melted him again. How could any man be so fortunate in love?

He buckled his belt, holstered his Remington over his white flannel nightshirt, and proceeded to the echoing door, playing his guessing game: doctor or sheriff?

Sheriff, he decided, and slid the Remington out as he drew the deadbolt back. Before him in the mustard-colored dawn stood, unsteady on his feet, Mordecai Sapp, the master of that hellhole up the river called Hogtown. A sheriff matter, then.

"I need some doctoring, Toole," rasped the man.

Santiago Toole peered closer into the shadowed dawn and saw the fat purveyor of all known vices leaning heavily on a staff of some sort, face drawn with fatigue and pain. And beside him Sapp's pet wolf, Popskull, with a bloody furrow across his skull.

"They've beaten you up again," said Toole. "A proper attitude, I suppose. Or is it one of your poor doxies? Have you come for one of them?"

Sapp shook his head and pushed in, limping heavily on a leg

3

that barely functioned. Popskull sulked outside. The master of Hogtown looked done in, all right. Toole nodded, slid his Remington home, and led the man into his office where umber shadows danced off green bottles and ivory skulls.

"Let me guess. Your tummy aches," Toole said, surveying the muddy, damp pants and purple chesterfield gambler duds.

"I've been shot in the head."

The sheriff side of Toole perked up at that. It happened all the time. A sheriff who was also a doctor had unusual means of discovering violent perforations of anatomy in his jurisdiction. It all intertwined amazingly.

"In the head, you say?"

Sapp pointed at a blood-blacked spot over his right ear. "It went in here and came out up here."

Doctor Toole, graduate of the University of Edinburgh School of Medicine, 1872, gasped.

"You are not dead," he whispered.

Mordecai Sapp fixed him in his oily eye. "Only the good die young."

Santiago Toole seated his patient in a bentwood rocker—a handy device to tip a patient on his ear, he'd found—and inspected the entry and exit holes. No doubt about it. A smaller one, perfectly round, just above this lecher's ear, right through the temporal, and a larger exit hole through the parietal, jagged-edged with shards of white bone, on the man's noggin. From the latter, a white gelatinous mass of brain bulged, mixed with a little blood.

"I suppose you committed suicide," Toole said shrewdly, following twin threads of sheriff and medical interest.

"Why would I do that? No, some of the troopers got a bit frisky."

Toole grunted. Lawing and medicine practiced jointly had kept his life continually absorbing. Medicine led to crime or crime led to medicine. Both of his callings profited. He was a better sheriff because he was a doctor. He liked to think he fought diseases not just in persons, but in the social order.

"I confess I'm not quite sure what to do. Living corpses are beyond my experience," he muttered. "I suppose some clean-

ing and carbolic and a plaster. I take it this has affected your
left limbs, eh?''

"Like a stroke, almost.''

"I don't think that bone will grow back. We'll have to
devise something to cover these holes, eh?'' he said, gently
dabbing away the filth—lots of mud, he noticed. Odd that there
should be wet mud. He held his lamp over the upper hole,
watching the throb of the living brain bulging up in it. "No
doubt there'll be some inflammation," he said. "We'd better
leave these holes open to reduce the pressure. Otherwise you'll
get stuff-headed and suffer."

"I thought about that. I'd like to have some corks put in."

"Corks! Corks! Sapp, they aren't sanitary and they'd tumble
out and your pudding brain would spoil."

"Whatever you say, doctor."

"You've got mud up here. Wet mud. Did these frisky troopers roll you in mud outside after murdering you?"

Sapp paused, studying Toole through lidded eyes. "Something like that."

"Have you reported your murder over at Fort Keogh?"

"Not yet."

"Are you going to?"

"Ah . . .'' Mordecai Sapp slid into silence. Santiago Toole
pulled brown hair out of the twin holes, cut away ragged folds
of scalp, making a neat circle, plucked shards of bone from the
upper one, delicately sawed off a splinter, tweezered away bits
of bullet lead, wiped the area with dilute carbolic, sprayed each
hole with a carbolic sprayer, and wondered whom to arrest.

"Let me see you walk,'' he said, after listening to the man's
heart with his stethoscope. "And do what you can with your
left arm."

The bulgy hooligan barely got out of the chair. Tremors
shook him. But he struggled up and lumbered heavily about the
small, cluttered office, making floorboards creak under his
mass.

"Will I get movement back?"

"How should I know? Maybe, when the fevers die down.
Brains are almost terra incognita to medicine. I think you got
shot through the base emotions."

Sapp settled into the groaning rocker again, and the chair lurched back and forward on its protesting runners.

"I'll put adhesive plasters on these now. Later, I'll make plates of gold or silver, which will be strong and noncorrosive. I'll anchor them under the scalp somehow. Scalp flesh should grow over them some, pinning them on."

"I got some eagles and double eagles. The dollies were holding out on me, but I got them." Sapp dug into his damp muddy pants and extracted the coins.

"Wages of sin," muttered Toole. "All right. I'll take some measurements here and begin hammering these into some plates."

"I have a headache, Toole."

"Fancy that! I'll give you some Dover's Powder. That's a good anodyne. I have three-grain doses. No more than twice a day, you understand. Have you had any spasms?"

"Dizzy, sort of."

"That's your normal condition. Let me know of any changes. Immediately."

"Yeah, sure. I'll be on my way. . . ."

"You're not going anywhere. Sit still! Who were these frisky troopers? What did they do? Start at the beginning. But first, were any others injured? The girls?"

"They're asleep," said Sapp somberly.

"That's a hell of an answer."

Sapp pondered. "It was a big, tough foreigner. A Turk or something. Never been there before. New to me. Didn't like losing at my monte game. No warning. I pulled in some chips and first thing I knew, he pulled a revolver and shot."

Toole sighed. "You're not convincing me."

"It's true!"

"The path of that bullet, which entered the side of your noggin, proceeds upward at about a forty-five-degree angle. As if you'd been shot while lying on your side on the ground or in bed, from someone firing from the foot of the bed."

"Take it or leave it."

"What did this Turk look like?"

"Dark. Very dark. Spade beard. Watery, intelligent eyes. Ears with little points on top. Broad-chested. Swarthy. Small horns coming from his skull, and cloven hoofs. Wearing red longjohns.''

The fat hog had a smirky look on him.

''Who witnessed it?''

''I was alone. This happened late, after the bar shut down and the dollies quit.''

''Alone! You're never alone. Where was that pox-faced moron of yours who pulls triggers and beats those poor girls for you?''

''He was asleep.''

''Why did you come alone? Injured and alone?''

''They were all asleep.''

''With holes in your head. Alone.''

Sapp shrugged. ''Can I go now?''

Toole glowered at him. ''I should lock you up as a material witness to your own murder. That'd be an interesting charge. Go. I'm riding out there shortly and talk to your floozies and thugs. You going back out there now?''

Mordecai Sapp remained silent.

''You'd better find a room in Miles, if you can wake up a night clerk. Maybe one's up now. In fact, I insist on it.''

Sapp smiled heavily. ''You want payment?''

''From you, always.''

They settled up, and Santiago Toole watched the swine lumber into the swallowing amber light of a sleeping town. Sapp trembled as he walked, leaning heavily on the staff he'd brought. The hope of more rest had vanished entirely, so Santiago settled into his rocker, working it furiously in his dark office, not knowing which excited his imagination more, his sheriff's duties or his medical ones. He had a case of attempted murder, unless the man put that bullet in his head himself, which seemed unlikely.

Nothing the big blob had said rang true.

Sheriff Santiago Toole had made a point of riding out to Hogtown fairly frequently. Within the grubby, cottonwood log buildings he'd discovered not only enlisted men from the Fort but a fine howling collection of riffraff, some of them wanted men. Wolfers. The last of the buffalo-runners. People running from the law: deserters, bank-robbers, and wife-stabbers. Paid killers and road agents. All the sorts who wanted redeye and harlots and privacy, well hidden from any settlement in the territory. He'd nabbed several men there, always at high risk from a glowering, hostile crowd, barkeeps who kept sawed-off shotguns handy, and that weird moron who did Sapp's rough stuff.

He had medical reasons, too, though he kept them well hidden from Sapp or his thugs. The women. The poor, desperate, diseased, dying, suicidal girls, trapped in a hell with no exit. Once he'd tried to spirit one out but she'd refused, preferring opium, laudanum, rotgut, and masochism to a new life. Some of the girls would have nothing to do with him, but two of them welcomed him, wept before him, confessed to him as if he were an Irish priest.

China Belle and Little Etta. China Belle's people were Cantonese, imported to build the railroads and then cast aside to scratch livings from gardens, laundering, and played-out gold digs. She'd been sold in San Francisco, sold again and again, and now Sapp owned her. Little Etta had been an immigrant girl, Bohemian, who'd run out of luck in the New World, and made the only living she could until she discovered it wasn't a living but slavery, and whatever she gained Sapp and others before him stole, whipping her for holding out on them.

These two especially welcomed him, and he did what he could, treating their syphilis with mercury and sometimes arsenic and bismuth; their pain with laudanum; their souls with listening and caring.

Fascinating the way lawing and medicine intertwined, he thought as he saddled his bay in the peach light of a June dawn. But sometimes they fought each other, too, especially when Sheriff Toole had to do things that troubled Dr. Toole. His passion for justice equaled his passion to heal. He intended to get there early, an unexpected hour. Wake up the ladies and start them jabbering. Look around before evidence vanished. He tightened the latigo, kneed the gelding, yanked the latigo again while the horse exhaled, and anchored the latigo on the cinch ring.

After carefully shaving with a well-stropped straightedge he had slipped into his black pin-striped trousers, shiny boots, white collarless shirt, and black vest with a steel star pinned on it. A black Irish, blue-eyed sheriff, slim younger son of a baron, now a minion of Yankee law. It pleased him. He'd flicked one of Mimi's long jet hairs from his trim vest and eyed her sleeping form fondly. He loved her. Next he'd clasped his black belt and holster with the Remington .44 in it. He kept spare rounds in his saddlebags. The left one toted his medical gear; the right one his sheriff's supplies, manacles, ammunition, field glasses, and emergency rations. He'd start with the ladies. They usually knew a lot, and they knew him for a healer and friend. The saloonkeepers would be tougher.

He snorted. At first, when they'd pinned the star on him, he'd wrestled with it. Shoot a felon and then doctor him? What of his Hippocratic Oath? He'd finally concluded it would be a matter of offices. In the office of sheriff, he'd shoot if he had to. Some men needed shooting—like Mordecai Sapp. Too bad that bullet hadn't sprayed lead into his whole brain. As doctor, he patched up the ones he shot. Very handy. He'd saved several carcasses for later hanging. The dexterity that made him a deft surgeon made him a swift man with a gun, and more importantly, an accurate one. So good, in fact, he often shot to wound, knowing precisely the intended effect. If he could call himself a pill-pusher, then he could push lead pills as well, in measured doses. A shot to the patella. A bullet into a gunman's metacarpal bones.

Here was attempted murder, and the murderee as silent as a tomb about it. A case. He might, of course, ride over to Fort Keogh about it. Maybe ask that top sergeant, Vernon Wiltz, who seemed to know most of what the officers there never found out. Yes, he'd do that. But not just yet. First he'd ride to Hogtown and probe a bit. Why had Sapp been so reluctant to talk? Afraid he'd lose trade if he squealed on some soldiers? Impossible. Hogtown honey always drew the bees. Revenge, maybe. Sapp might be planning his own pill party to get even. Or maybe just shock. People with holes in their heads aren't inclined to be chatty.

A case to write about, he thought. A fine *Lancet* piece. A man who'd been shot in the head and left part of his brain splattered all over his saloon had walked into his office. A novelty. Something to share with those addled Yankee officers at Keogh, who played croquet and waltzed with each other's wives and massacred antelope now that the Sioux had slowed their renegading. Not that the country had become safe. Sitting Bull and other irreconcilables lurked in Canada. Whole bands of bitter young Sioux broncos jumped the reservations every summer, just about now in fact, looking for white men to slaughter. Especially buffalo-runners. The Sioux hated the hide-hunters even more than soldiers, knowing what had happened to the southern herd and what it portended for their free nomadic life.

He rode west from Miles, past the quiet fort upslope, frame buildings around a parade, and on toward Hogtown as the morning light blued the sky and hued a gray world. The low sun silvered the river and cast a long shadow before him. Surprise. One of the best tactics in a sheriff's kit bag. Few people had ever seen Hogtown by daylight. It purveyed its wares by the black of the night, lit by lanterns and candles or not lit at all. He'd usually come by day, while its denizens slept. It lay under cottonwoods in a gulch bottom, the main building a rectangle of silvery-gray cottonwood logs with a pole and sod roof overhead. The rough saloon in front had no windows at all, and by day seemed singularly gloomy. But nights it glowed evil yellow from smoking lanterns that burned buffalo tallow. At the rear were the ladies' cribs, narrow cubicles with nothing but a rough bedstead and cornshuck or bunchgrass pad, and a worn robe or blanket or two. These also lacked light, except for whatever sun leaked through the chinks. A rock and mud-mortar fireplace in the saloon provided the only heat. The women had no doors; only a rough curtain of ancient blanket nailed over holes in the log walls. Sapp liked it that way: No dolly had secrets from him.

Santiago Toole focused on these things as he steered his bay through muck and puddles from the night's deluge on a river trail worn smooth by the boots of soldiers. Even by daylight he'd had to light candles to treat these poor women in their dungeons. Give them sun, give them air, he'd once told Sapp, but Sapp had retorted that sun would give them notions. The king of Hogtown himself lived separately in a cottonwood log cabin with a covered porch. A lean-to at the rear was home for that pox-faced killer and bodyguard called Herold. A few scruffy outbuildings completed the hog ranch. By day, one could ride by it and see only a rude settlement that bespoke nothing of the carmined hell within.

His best bet, he thought, would be to slip into the big building quietly and talk with Belle or Etta without stirring up anyone else. That'd take a little doing. Horses might whicker. Roustabouts might be up and doing such few chores as Sapp forced upon them. That weird menace Herold might skulk about at any hour of day or night. Just before rounding the last shoulder of bluff, Santiago Toole pulled his field glasses from his bag. Then he left the worn trail and rode upslope, cutting the corner. Juniper shrubbery and jack pines on the slope above would conceal an observer, he thought, and he could study the squalid dump for as long as he wished.

He touched his boots and reined the bay left, sensing the horse's resistance to leaving a familiar trail. But it clambered up a slope roughened by dun sandstone outcrops, and then up the east side of the shoulder, topping it three or four hundred yards above Hogtown. There Toole paused, dropped the knotted reins over the pommel, and focused his glass. When at last the image leapt past several intervening cottonwoods in new lime leaf, it reached into a charred mass. Hogtown, burnt to the ground! Startled, Sheriff Toole glassed the rest of the compound. Sapp's house a mass of ash. Some rough sheds standing. Everything rain-drenched.

Burnt to earth! A blaze well concealed by the surrounding bluffs and ridges! Being a cautious man, and more aware than other lawmen what a hundred fifty or two hundred grains of lead might do to his anatomy, he glassed the surrounding country grimly, studying squat olive-colored junipers and lemon-colored outcrops of stratified rock. Nothing.

Burnt! Not a sign of life. This thing somehow connected with Sapp's wound. Where was everyone? Escaped, no doubt. Chased into the night by fire or vengeful soldiers or maybe even renegade Indians. Cautiously he glassed the ashes once again and then touched boot heel to the bay's flanks and jarred roughly downslope into Hogtown, or what remained of it. Broken green bottle glass. Bits of metal. The stone and mud hearth erect. He dismounted quietly in the soft zephyrs of early morning and walked through the powdery gray and black ash, studying, mastering, hunting down the elusive somethings that would give him a clue—any sort of clue—about the night's calamities. Nothing.

There were no bodies and that seemed a good sign. Puddles still standing. This fire had burned before the deluge obviously. He could follow water-washed streaks of ash downslope, see pools of gritty water standing among piles of char. Too late to save anything. He hunted for telltale signs of brown oxidized blood, but the rain had swept the area clean. Hail, too, no doubt. Downslope a bit in the bottom of the coulee, where the grasses had been flattened by a flash flood, he spotted a curious depression of raw earth, with soaked shapeless mounds of excavated clay beside it. He walked downslope swiftly, sensing something important there. The shallow hollow, perhaps four feet by six, had filled with smooth tan mud, still more liquid than solid. He poked a twig into it and felt the stick slide easily through the muck. A grave? Or what? The disturbed earth lay perhaps a hundred yards above the Yellowstone River on a steep grade that more or less paralleled the trail in from Fort Keogh.

Whatever had happened here, he sensed that this mud-filled depression had something to do with it. He hunted for a spade in the unburnt sheds and found an ancient one with a broken handle. It'd do. He returned to the strange depression and began shoveling the slop out, regretting that he'd worn his professional clothes. Heavy work. Each shovelful was weighted with the burden of cold water. And he got nothing at all for his sweated labor. An hour later, wearied by fruitless toil, he gave up. He'd struck undisturbed earth and rock a couple or three feet down, maybe more. If anything had been in this pit—bodies for instance—that flood must have washed it all into the river.

With that as a surmise, he trudged downslope over the watercourse, finding nothing. Not a scrap of snagged cloth; not a coin or belt. The water had ripped through a muddy hollow and out into the gray river, turbid with the dun rainwash it carried. Nothing. Maybe it had been nothing more than a new sanitary trench. He stared into the racing river, running hard and mean between distant creamy bluffs, and decided that if Sapp had secrets, they'd vanished in the flood.

He felt sure of nothing. Still, he sensed death. Sapp had a bullet hole in his brain. Something had happened here and the rain had wiped away every trace. He turned back to the ruins, and saw four blue-shirted riders approaching on the trail from Fort Keogh.

Chapter 2

Sergeant Major Vernon Wiltz knew who ran the army. Those high above him thought they did, but they were wrong. Top sergeants ran the army. He and his kind could make or break an officer and did not hesitate to do so. A little zeal, a little resistance, a little subterfuge. Sweeping things under the rug. A careful suggestion or two, offered in such a way that the officer thought it was his own idea. And above all, quietly handling the ugly personnel problems that officers rarely bothered with, but which could erupt at any time into big trouble.

Such as Keogh's morale and health problems, not to mention its appalling desertion rate and the occasional disappearance of a soldier who hadn't deserted. They were easy to spot. Deserters usually stole their Springfield rifles and other gear when they went over the hill. Others simply vanished. Little troubles cropped up—disobedience, rebellion, theft of government property, murder, mayhem. Half the frontier army was fresh off the immigrant boats; the other half was escaping an unsavory past.

Sergeant Major Wiltz dealt with them all. Not a man on the post could beat him in a brawl. Usually one punch from his ham hands would topple even the meanest brute of a soldier. Vernon Wiltz had an ox-build: massive shoulders and hard gut, a bullet head almost naked of hair except for a brown ridge of it over the ears, and a bull neck as thick as his head. Depending on the season and his mood, his flesh ran from bright pink to purple, tending toward brown late summers.

That little party at Hogtown the night before had been one of

14

those things sergeants major do and never explain. The filthy place had sucked the health and wealth of Fort Keogh down to nothing. A third of his Fifth Infantry garrison on sick call, usually with clap, syphilis, ague, consumption, and sometimes the aftereffects of opium, not to mention poisonous red-eye. On the average, a third. But that was only the beginning. Keogh had lost tens of thousands of dollars of gear, swiped by enlisted men to trade for gambling chips at Sapp's crooked tables. Everything vanished: cartridges, rifles, revolvers, knapsacks, blankets, ponchos, McClellan saddles, tack, boots, hats, blouses, britches, messware, knives, haversacks, cartridge belts, bayonets. Once a barracks stove. All that plus the whole post payroll each and every month. They blew their thirteen dollars on rotgut, a woman, and a few hands of monte. And when they'd shot their wad, they traded blouses and boots for more and got docked for it.

That hasn't been the end of it either, he thought. Fort Keogh had a nine percent-a-year desertion rate, and Hogtown was usually the first stop on the way over the hill. Keogh was a hardship post, in spite of a good library and reading room, a dance hall and chapel for the enlisted men. But yonder lay Hogtown, where a deserter could trade everything he had for a few greenbacks and get out. Or be killed. Sergeant Major Wiltz knew but couldn't prove that the denizens of Hogtown simply murdered troopers now and then, especially if they caused trouble, and dumped their weighted bodies into the Yellowstone River somewhere. It maddened him that he couldn't prove it. He'd set a few good men spying over there and they'd come up with nothing. But Wiltz knew it. He knew that the pox-faced punk over there enjoyed pumping lead into a soldier, just as Mordecai Sapp enjoyed stripping the remains of every last valuable.

The truth of it was that Fort Keogh lay weak, its strength halved by the hemorrhage into Hogtown. Given another Sioux uprising, the return of Sitting Bull, troubles such as the recent Bannock war or the earlier flight of the Nez Percé, Keogh would lie helpless. Its commanding officer, Colonel Orville Prescott Wade, scarcely understood and didn't want to know. Its captains and lieutenants busied themselves with theatrical productions, quartermaster duties, afternoon tea, and literary society readings. That left the problem to the sergeant major and his loyal noncoms, who ran Keogh anyway.

Which is how it had happened that Sergeant Major Wiltz took matters into his own hands, organized a cabal of battle-hardened noncoms who wouldn't shrink from the hard task, and dealt death to Hogtown early the previous morning. They'd slipped in just after the joint had shut down, shot the four males, herded the girls out to a common grave and shot them, and torched the place. There'd been some hitches. That poxy punk Herold hadn't died easily, and put a bullet into Corporal Horn. The deluge cut short the burying and put the fires out too soon. And they'd recovered no government-issue gear. Sapp apparently shipped it out as fast as he got hold of it. But no matter. The hellhole was now ash and its stinking inmates were cold meat.

There were, of course, odds and ends. Breaking the news to the officers. Organizing an inquiry, for the record. A daylight trip to examine the site. This would have two purposes. The official one would be informational; a report to the CO. The unofficial one would be to make sure no evidence had been left behind; to cover their tracks, clear his little cabal of all blame. He'd chosen his men with care, and knew every soldier to keep a secret. He'd enforced the silence with his personal guarantee that he'd butcher anyone who opened his big mouth, drunk or sober. But he wasn't worried about that. These were all career army, wanting promotions, and the recommendations all just happened to flow across his desk.

He found Colonel Wade at his golden oak desk, reading a new Ned Buntline dime novel about Buffalo Bill Cody.

"Yes, Sergeant?" he said, peering up behind gold-rimmed spectacles.

"Colonel, sah, I have word that Hogtown burned last night. Before the storm."

Wade grinned. "Good riddance."

"I agree, sah. I'm thinking maybe a party of noncoms should ride over to have a look. Maybe find out what happened. Maybe find out who's there. Maybe recover post property, sah."

Colonel Wade mulled it, wrinkling the formidable frown lines across his brow to convey thought to his observer. "Yes," he said after an appropriate interval. "Yes. Find what you can. If one of our men burnt it, we'll have to discipline him—destroying property and all that."

"I'll have to deal with that scoundrel Sapp. He'll raise a ruckus and want money, I suppose. Find out what happened to the inmates. If any died, there'll be trouble from the civilian authorities, I imagine. But of course, I think you'll find no connection between the fire and Fort Keogh. It might have been an accident."

"Probably an accident, sah. I plan to go myself and take three. That means putting Buford in my slot a few hours. I'll arrange it, sah."

"I think I'll send an officer with you. Just in case . . ."

"Sah, no officer's even been in that hellhole. I don't think, sah, that an officer would be helpful. Noncoms know what to look for, if you'll pardon my sayin' so."

"Very good. How'd you find out?"

"Corporal Diggs, sah. He saw the fire."

"Well, get a statement from him. You know, Vernon, this is a fine thing. What'll the men think?"

"The troops, sah, aren't paid to think."

"Ah! Right you are. They'll find other ways to squander their pay. In Miles, I suppose. Well, get to it, and report to me afterward."

It had been easy. He'd posted Sergeant Chester Buford, one of his cabal, to his own office. Then he'd gathered up his corporals, gotten horses from the cavalry stables, and ridden off on a fine sunny morning, wet with the puddles of the dawn deluge.

Behind him rode Corporals Horn, Liggett, and Polanc, all silent and sleep-robbed, and none of them happy to return to a murder site. Each of them, Wiltz knew, had butchered a girl and felt haunted by it. War was one thing; murdering women another. That's why he'd posted them to this detail. He'd rub their soldier noses in it when they got there. The frontier world didn't take kindly to the slaughter of women; not even these worn-out, diseased dollies. He'd hold it over them, this terrible secret of theirs.

That delighted Sergeant Major Wiltz. He loved levers. He had all sorts of levers, even on officers. Such as the two elderly lieutenants he'd caught converting government property into private wealth. He twisted around in his saddle and studied the faces of these conspirators, reading them one by one. Then he smiled. His sorrel horse sidled under the shifting weight.

"You know what to look for. Anything of interest, Horn, see if Sapp had any horses or mules and collect them. Polanc, I want your eyes to the ground. Look for anything of interest around the grave. Liggett, you search the outbuildings for anything of interest, and walk up the coulee looking for caches of hot goods."

No one answered. The borrowed cavalry mounts slopped through silver puddles and skidded on wet, dun gumbo as the detail rode silently through a lively morning, freshened by June zephyrs. They rounded the last massive shoulder of river bluff and beheld the Hogtown coulee, steaming warmly. Beyond some cottonwoods the charred mound lay sullen and soaked. A few sheds sagged desolately. Bright black and white magpies hopped raucously from limb to limb, following the soldiers. And below the ruins, down near the muddy grave, stood a tall man in black pin-striped pants, white collarless shirt, and black vest, with a sidearm strapped to his hip.

Astonished, Wiltz halted his troop and stared, even while the young man stared back. Then the sergeant major understood, or at least had some inkling. The steel star glinting on the distant man's vest told him that Sheriff Toole was prowling around the ruins. Wiltz didn't like that a bit. Especially not this early, only a few hours after it had all happened.

He touched boot heel to the sorrel and trotted forward, taking in everything, especially the grave, which showed signs of tampering, fresh watery slop piled at its side. Curious, he rode directly for the grave, aware of Toole's brilliant blue eyes following him. Wiltz peered over the neck of the sorrel into the shallow pit and saw . . . nothing. A sea of dun muck, a waterlogged hole gouged into it. Nothing. He smiled faintly.

"Morning, Sheriff."

Toole nodded, his thoughtful gaze scanning each of the noncoms.

"What brings you here?" Wiltz persisted, faint belligerence in his tone.

"I might ask you the same thing, Sergeant."

Wiltz ignored the question. "You learn something about this?"

"I did. And what did you learn, Sergeant?"

It annoyed him. Sergeant Major Wiltz wasn't used to being questioned.

"What have you found, Sheriff?" he demanded. He had a way of intimidating men with his rough, gravely voice; a way of thrusting himself forward, of menacing. He employed that familiar tactic now.

"It seems to have burned," Toole said amiably, revealing nothing.

"How'd you find out about this?"

"Why . . . Mr. Sapp told me."

Toole's sapphire eyes lit with amusement, watching Wiltz's response. And Wiltz, in turn, barely concealed his astonishment.

"Ah! That's a good one, Sheriff."

"Why do you say that? And what brings you here, Sergeant Wiltz?"

"We'd a report—" Wiltz began and clammed up. What the hell business was it of the sheriff? "Mordecai Sapp isn't the sort to go to a sheriff."

"He didn't come for a sheriff; he came for a doctor."

Some wild emotion exploded in Wiltz. He remembered Toole practiced medicine, too. Fears raced through him, curiosity, and skepticism. Imagine Sapp coming for a doctor after being buried with a pair of holes in his skull. Wiltz laughed nastily, not daring to say a word. Why the hell was this fancy doctor-sheriff here, and fitting a hangman's noose over their necks? He suppressed an itch to leap from his sorrel and strangle Toole with his own bare hands. But this would take diplomacy, something all sergeants major were well stocked with. He smiled crookedly.

"Good riddance, eh? The army's better off without this hellhole, and I imagine you folks in Miles feel the same way."

"I'm wondering what happened. Aren't you curious, Sergeant? What happened to the women?"

"Hadn't thought much about that. They ain't worth much. We heard about the fire and came over looking for government property. A lot's missing over there."

"I intend to find out."

"Aw, Sheriff, this dump . . . these low-lifes ain't worth the effort." Sergeant Wiltz decided the time had come to take command here, and turned to his corporals. "Start looking. You find any army things, come get me."

His corporals dismounted and spread out, except for Polanc, who hovered near the pit.

"You won't find government property in a mudhole, Polanc," he said sharply. "Poke around those sheds."

Sheriff Toole watched them go, and then turned to Wiltz. "Maybe there's been a crime here, maybe not. I want to see what they find. If it doesn't belong to the army, it stays here."

Wiltz noted a bite to the man's voice, and swallowed back his own rage and contempt.

"Sheriff, this here's army business. This here place sucked blood from my boys, and stole Fort Keogh blind. We'll just take care of this. Whatever happened, we'll figure it out and deal with it. Agreed?"

"No." Toole was actually grinning at him, his direct gaze steady on Wiltz's face. The sergeant felt himself reddening, as he always did when provoked.

"Well then I'm telling you, Sheriff. Stay out."

"This place isn't on the military reservation. It's in my county. Its inmates are—or were—civilians. It had army trade, but it also had civilian trade. Lots of buffalo-runners here. Some riffraff. I've pulled wanted men out of here—all civilian. And I intend to find out what happened. Sorry, Wiltz."

"You heard me, Sheriff."

Toole shrugged. "Tamper with any evidence and I'll have a talk with Colonel Wade, Sergeant."

Vernon Wiltz watched silently as the sheriff resumed digging in the slop-filled pit, lifting oozing muck from its bottom. The work fascinated Wiltz. There'd been a flash flood down these bottoms. The flattened grass told the story. It'd rolled over the shallow grave, apparently sluicing away the clay they'd thrown over the bodies. Maybe even washed them down to the river, down the steep slope. Startled, he thought of something.

"You say Sapp came to you, looking for a doc?" he asked blandly.

Toole looked up at him. "Sapp was injured."

"What kind of injury?"

"I don't discuss the medical problems of my patients."

Wiltz burned. "What're you looking for in that pit?"

"Bodies." Toole leaned on the old spade, his gaze following the blue-bloused corporals who roamed over the coulee poking and probing.

"Looks like a sanitary pit or a garbage pit to me."

"Yes, it does," Toole said amiably. "But it's freshly dug. The grass in those clumps of sod is green and alive. Maybe dug last night before this fire. Something connects this pit to that fire."

"Is that what Sapp told you?"

Toole smiled. "Sapp didn't say much."

Then Wiltz knew. The answer hit him. The damned flood had rolled the stiffs out of that grave and into the river. That mound of blubber, Sapp, must have floated like a buoy. His body probably snagged down river somewhere and was found and reported. Toole would have noted the bullet holes in Sapp's brain and ridden over here. Thanks to the goddamn storm, Toole was sniffing around with a murder case, and maybe getting close to something.

"So Sapp wanted a doc. Alive, huh?"

"Quite alive, Sergeant."

The sheriff did some fancy lying, Wiltz thought. Had he found any other bodies? "What do you figure happened to his dollies, Sheriff? And those barkeeps of his? And that scum he kept around?"

"Perhaps you know better than I, Sergeant."

Toole had a way of turning the questions about that nonplussed Wiltz. He felt the heat boil through him again. He'd crush this immigrant mick like a bug if he had to.

Wiltz grinned. "Looks like we both want some answers, Toole."

"Care to dig?" Toole shoved the spade into Wiltz's paws. The sergeant pitched the shovel to earth, as if it were a scalding iron.

"Naw!"

"You have less curiosity than I do, Sergeant. Perhaps you know something I don't. Such as the contents of this pit before the flood washed them into the Yellowstone."

Far up the coulee Cletus Horn led a gray horse downslope, catching the sheriff's stare. Toole studied the other corporals as they poked and probed through the outlying sheds. Horn led the horse, a ribby animal that had gone untended, up to Vernon Wiltz.

"All I could find."

"We'll take it."

"I don't see the U.S. brand on it, Sergeant. Unless you can show me that it's army property, it stays here."

"Toole, I told you to stay out of this. But you don't listen."

Toole nodded. "I heard you," he said softly. "Colonel Wade will hear of it, too. I'll discuss a lot of things, including your remarkable lack of curiosity about what went on here sometime before the storm last night."

Sergeant Major Wiltz hadn't been addressed like this within memory. He'd always hated civilians, and this tall, stern, watchful one with a doctor's sheepskin and a fancy steel star on his skinny chest he hated worst of all. The bastard needed teaching.

"Saddle up!" he barked to his corporals. "We're done here. Found out what we wanted. Horn, lead that horse."

He watched while his men mounted. All of them glanced furtively at him, caution in their faces.

"Go. I'll catch up."

They trotted off. He turned toward Toole. "You didn't listen, Toole. So I have to show you. Stay out of this. Don't even stick your nose in army business again."

He edged in close, feeling heat bull through his body. Toole didn't move, sucker that he was. Wiltz cocked his huge fist and cut upward, smashing Toole just under the rib cage, a blow to the solar plexus that could kill a man. In fact, Wiltz had killed two men like that. Men who couldn't breathe, couldn't make their diaphragms work afterward. Toole gasped and crumpled in a heap, folding up over his shocked gut. The sheriff spasmed on the ground, his mouth a sucking circle, limbs convulsing. Wiltz watched him, feeling the first satisfaction he'd known since encountering the man. The nosy sheriff wasn't breathing, and maybe wouldn't again.

Cheerfully, Wiltz hoisted himself into the saddle. He was infantry, not cavalry, but made a point of mastering everything, including men and horses.

If Toole lives, he thought, he'll never mess with the army again. Sergeants major have their ways.

Chapter 3

The blow caught Santiago Toole by surprise. It rammed the air out of his lungs and he couldn't fill them up again. He folded to earth, paralyzed, feeling hot hurt lash out from his belly. He gasped for air, tried to suck it in, but nothing worked. Not a muscle in his body contracted. Even his heart spasmed. He saw white, only white, pulsing white. From some vast distance he heard a gravelly voice.

"I told you," it said.

Then nothing. Desperate for air he convulsed, some muscles spasming at last in a death dance. No air. No bellows. The white danced, pulsed before his closed eyes, and then faded as the agony persisted. He longed for air, for just one big gulp, but his lungs refused to draw air. He felt himself sliding into oblivion and then remembered nothing. . . .

Some while later he regained awareness. His lungs were working rhythmically but with deep, angry pain where Wiltz's fist had smashed into him. Air. He groaned dizzily, aware of life. Heart slamming irregularly. Lungs wheezing. Weakness. Too weak to lift a limb, his whole body flattened upon wet grass as heavily as death itself. Time passed—he had no idea how much—and gradually his mind began collecting vagrant thoughts, feathery and muddled.

Holy Mary . . . a killer punch . . . blow to the solar plexus . . . the kind that murdered . . . from Wiltz. . . .

Strands of rage wove together in him, and among them the red thread of terror. He'd never taken a killer blow like that; premeditated murder. Sergeant Major Vernon Wiltz had meant to kill him or terrorize him, one or the other. He thought of shooting Wiltz. He thought of running, running, to the end of the earth to escape a man who could do that, who could paralyze his body with a single punch.

He rolled to his side, panting, sweaty, nauseated, wanting to vomit. But the red pain in his gut somehow kept him from spilling his bile upon the earth. He'd kill Wiltz or be killed. A dozen anatomy lessons crowded into him then: the dense cluster of nerve cells and ganglia just under the diaphragm, near the celaic artery, behind the stomach. A blow there could stop visceral functioning. Men like Wiltz knew the effect, if not the cause, of an uppercut there.

He chose to sleep, and drifted through the mid-morning into noon before he finally sat up, awakened by crows who lined a cottonwood limb near him, eyeing carrion. When he stirred, they flapped off in a raucous black crowd. He stood. Except for a heaviness, he felt normal. He peered about, fearful of Wiltz, and drew out his Remington .44. But not a soul lingered around the ruin of Hogtown. He slid the weapon back, ashamed of the terror that had exploded in him and wondering if he could ever face Wiltz. He had to. Face Wiltz or run and keep on running.

Noon, he thought, squinting into the glare of the sky. He studied the mud smearing his black pin-striped trousers and black vest. The same gumbo he'd seen on Sapp, the mud he'd gently washed out of Sapp's wounds. Toole wandered over to the pit, staring into it. Dun gumbo clay. The stuff smeared his steel star. Tenderly he unpinned it and wiped it until it shone, until no tarnish marred this ensign of office. Then he pinned it on again, an act fraught with meaning. He might be a younger son of an Irish lord, but the office he held in this young republic commanded every fiber of his loyalty and skill. He would be a sheriff, and he'd bring the killers to justice, Wiltz or no Wiltz.

He walked stiffly toward the water-soaked mound of char, convinced that murder had been done here, soldiers had done it, and Wiltz knew something of it and approved. That would account for the way the sergeant had warned him off and then resorted to . . . an attempt at murdering the sheriff of Custer County.

He poked through the mess, not knowing what to look for

but studying everything with an intelligent eye, letting his imagination work. Broken glass, square nails, and then two sawed-off shotguns, stocks burnt away, barrels twisted from heat. The ones under the bar. Lying where the bar had been, unused. He supposed that told him something. No resistance. The thing had come after-hours, after the night's trade had left and Hogtown had settled into its sordid sleep.

How would it have been done? It would have required enough men to jump the two burly barkeeps, that pox-faced moron, and Sapp himself—the four armed men on the place. If they had jumped all four simultaneously, that meant at least four men, probably more. Yes, jump the four armed men first; the women later, at their leisure. He wasn't sure where the barkeeps slept, but it was somewhere in the main building, near the girls. Maybe even in the saloon. He'd check that out later. He knew where the other two slept. Sapp had his own cabin, and that killer kid had a lean-to room at its rear, where he could hover close protecting his fat master.

Santiago Toole abandoned the ruin of the main building and trudged wearily to the ashes of the cabin, wanting only to go to bed, tired beyond anything his young body had experienced. But a combined rage and pain drove him on, mixed with an icy desire to do justice to his office. He stared at the mess, noting the blackened frame of a brass bedstead. What had once been a mattress of some kind was only a soggy charred mass now, still resting on metal spring webbing. Sapp lived in virtual luxury compared to his slaves, Toole thought. Near the head of the bed he discovered a flattened, half-melted lead bullet, almost lost in the remains of a log wall. It figured. Someone had shot Sapp while he rested. Apparently before he undressed for bed. The bullet had exited from his head and smacked into the log wall, probably burying itself in wood until the fire released it. He pocketed the bullet. Its flat base was intact, and he'd measure its caliber when he returned to Miles. Cartridge ammunition, not a ball. Revolver round, probably.

Nothing else remained. Sapp's wardrobe had vanished; his dresser had burned, along with a small desk and whatever lay within it. Disappointed, Toole stepped around to the lean-to that had sheltered the punk. The killers would have started with him, killed the fastest and most dangerous of them first, he thought. But he found little that meant anything. Broken glass from a window; busted ceramic washbowl and pitcher, shards of mirror—the kid had been something of a dandy, he remembered. Shooters were like that, all prettied up for murder.

He could scarcely tell where the wooden bedstead had been, but he located it in a corner, flat against the main log wall of Sapp's cabin, now reduced to char. There, where the log wall had been, he found three more spent bullets. Similar to the one he'd found at Sapp's bed. So they jumped the kid, Herold, and took no chances, he thought. The bullets all lay buried near the corner, about where the kid's head and chest probably had been. He dug them out of floor and log and pocketed them.

The outlines of a massacre had formed in his head by then, and he headed back to the main building to look for lead in the cribs. Slowly he sifted through the ash, concentrating especially on China Belle's miserable room, and Little Etta's, finding nothing. Either the inferno had melted the lead until it ran into the ground somewhere below, or else the girls had been herded somewhere and shot. The thought of it, of their terror and screams, sent a shiver through him. They would have been last, and would have known of their fate before they died.

The hot sun was drying the mud on his clothing until it flaked off. He felt exhausted and wanted to sleep away the afternoon. He'd forgotten his bay, and for a moment couldn't find it, his mind boiling with dark accusation. Holy Mary, had Wiltz stolen his gelding, too? But then he spotted the animal far up the coulee where some grass remained, there being little edible around Hogtown.

When he reached the animal he caught it and pulled away the mess of slimy yellow grass that had collected on its bit as it grazed. It had broken a rein, but enough remained so that he could steer the animal, leaning forward a bit. A fine horse, a thoroughbred he'd imported to tickle his Irish fancy. St. James, he'd named the glowing animal, an anglicized version of the name, Santiago, his whimsical father had bestowed on him. He hadn't a drop of Spanish blood in him, but his name had led people to suppose he did.

He rode wearily home, wanting only to sleep, following the

trail east along the river flats, stripped of all wood to feed the Fort; past Keogh back from the river and to the south, on a plain above its floods. Its whitewashed, clapboard buildings glared brilliant under an azure heaven. On a distant meadow, blue-bloused soldiers drilled. He rode on into Miles, a town changing daily, prettying up its buildings with false fronts now that sawn wood had become plentiful. A whole block of stores squatted across Main, an enormously wide street: saloons and mercantiles and outfitters for troopers and buffalo-hunters, along with a sprawl of houses ranging from crude cabins to new gingerbreaded ones. Texas longhorns were on the way here up the Tongue River, they'd heard, and the whole village was calcimining itself for the bonanza. That and the arrival of the Northern Pacific next year. Already the merchants were calling the place Miles City, in anticipation. City it would be.

He turned into his own yard and unsaddled the gelding, turning it into its stall in the barn at the rear. Mimi met him at the door, looking dazzling as always, dressed today in lemon and white dimity, with her jet hair, the product of French and Assiniboin genes, loose over her shoulders. Her liquid doe-eyes surveyed him, pausing at his face and muddied trousers.

"Oh, Santiago! What happened?"

"Ran into a fist," he said wearily, settling in the sunny kitchen.

"You're hurt!" She came to him with soft golden hands, caressing his brow, running a hand over his unshaven cheeks and chin. "Tea," she added, turning to the kettle on the cold stove. It would take time.

He sagged in the wooden chair, watching her slender back and the way the loose hair rolled back and forth over her shoulders as she moved.

"They left a message here," she said, her back still to him. "But it can wait."

"Who?"

"Sylvane Tobias. They pulled a woman from the river. Naked and shot dead. She's over in the icehouse."

"Who?"

"They say one of the ones at Hogtown. A Chinese."

She turned to him, seeing the desolation in his face.

"I'm sorry," she whispered. "She was one of the ones you hoped to save."

Her gentle hands caressed him again, riding over his shoulders until he found himself drawing strength from her love.

"Mr. Tobias said he wouldn't do anything, no box or anything, until you got there. Just keep her on ice. He'll charge the county."

"No he won't," he said roughly. "I'm going to pay him myself."

"I'll have tea when you get back. And some lunch."

"Not hungry." He rose wearily, avoiding her gaze.

He found Sylvane Tobias in his cabinetmaking shop, planing an oak plank. The ruddy artisan set down the plane and without a word trudged out the back of his workroom toward a low log building at the rear, which housed block ice buried in a mountain of sawdust. One of his three enterprises, the other two being cabinetmaking and undertaking, since rude Milestown lacked a proper one. Sheriff Toole followed silently, knowing what to expect.

Tobias unlatched a massive gray-plank door and led the sheriff through a foot-thick boarded double wall packed with sawdust, into a russet gloom, with only sunlight from the open door lighting the way. A rough muslin sheet covered a slim form spread on ice where sawdust had been pushed away. The sheriff gently lifted the sheet, finding gray nakedness underneath and the stillness of death. China Belle. Two blue bullet wounds, one through her left breast, one in the belly. The river had washed the blood away. The chest wound probably had caught her heart or the mass of vessels and arteries just below it. The other hole, just under the sternum, probably pierced her stomach and might have damaged her spinal cord. Both fatal.

He stared at the holes in once-golden flesh, and into her remote face, which had settled into repose, eyes closed. Younger now, much younger than when he'd seen her alive. She hadn't lived long, perhaps twenty-five years at the most. But trapped in Sapp's cesspool she'd looked older, duller, decaying daily. He sighed.

"I have to turn her over," he said.

Tobias nodded, and together they lifted her stiff body until he could see her back and buttocks. Two exit holes, larger and ragged and mean, showing purple flesh within them.

"All right," he said shortly. They restored her to her back. If a bullet had lodged in her, he wanted it.

"No, wait," he said to Tobias, who held the sheet.

Caught in her nose lay a clot of dun gumbo mud. He peered closely at it. He found more buried in her ears, and some in her mouth when he firmly pried open the resisting flesh.

He nodded and Tobias briskly lowered the sheet over her.

"Find something there?"

"They were all dumped in a common grave that washed out."

"There were others?"

"Yes, Mr. Tobias."

The gray-eyed cabinetmaker stared expectantly at Toole, but the sheriff declined to talk. Didn't feel like talking.

"Are you done with her? She'll keep a few days in here."

"I'm done."

"I'll make a pine box and bury her then. It'll cost the county a little."

"Make an oak box. Gather every daisy on the hills and cover her with yellow. And plan a service when you're ready. I'll pay."

"A service. For a Chinawoman? What kind? Who'll come?" Sylvane Tobias looked worried.

"I'll come and I'll read. Mimi will come."

Tobias nodded. "You haven't asked what happened, Sheriff."

"Someone found her snagged on the river. Who, and what time?"

"The Mulligan boy. He was prowling around bright and early, before his mother was even up, saw her and came scooting to me. I fished her out a mile down. Maybe six or seven."

Toole nodded. "We'll look for others."

"All? All of Hogtown dead, Sheriff? Murdered like this?"

Toole paused, contemplating a lie, and then settled for a smaller one. "I don't know," he muttered. A quarter-truth. He believed they all were dead.

"I guess you'll tell me more when you're ready," Tobias

said, a bit grouchily. The man liked private information from the sheriff of Custer County.

"When I'm ready," Toole agreed as they emerged into dazzling sunlight that hurt his eyes. Behind him, Tobias carefully swung the massive door closed on squeaking hinges and dropped its hook into the eye. "Thank you, Sylvane," Toole added absently.

Find Sapp. He wandered into the mud-puddled broad street, scarcely aware that his own grimed clothing was drawing stares from several rough men and one parlorhouse woman. Find Sapp. Doctor Toole and Sheriff Toole both wanted Sapp. Not a difficult task in a rowdy buffalo town with three hundred fifty people, three hotels, twenty saloons, and three parlorhouses ranging in quality. They boasted there were more bawds than saloons in Miles, and more thieves and footpads than anywhere else in the West. And Santiago knew them all. But first he'd try the hotels. He picked the Northern, a long squat building of logs snaking rearward behind a clapboard false front calcimined white.

"You register someone early this morning?"

"No, Sheriff. No one since last night," said the boozy-breathed day clerk.

Toole swung the register around and studied its last entries. "This would have been around six. Night clerk still on?"

"No clerk then. I'm it, morning to midnight."

With little trips to the saloon next door, Toole thought. "I'm looking for Sapp. Hogtown Sapp. If you see him—"

"I'd never let him in here."

"Sure," said Toole.

Another place, at the west edge of town, seemed less likely. It consisted of a saloon-eatery below, and a large dormitory above, full of bedbug-ridden ticks. Buffalo-runners patronized it. That one was easy to check. He pushed past the surly, wall-eyed clerk with moles on his jowls, and bounded lightly up into the common sleeping room, which lay empty and fetid. No Sapp.

Back on mud-rutted Main Street, afternoon sun blinded him after he'd prowled the airless, gloomy flophouse. What remained? The Nelson Miles Hotel, too fancy for Sapp. A couple of boarding houses run by respectable women who would have refused Sapp on sight. He decided to ignore them for the moment. Twenty saloons, most of them narrow, one-story affairs stretching back from the street. All were open for the afternoon trade. He plunged into one and then another, waiting for his eyes to adjust to their thick umber shadows while sour beer odors assaulted his nostrils and grim barkeeps glared. Nothing but the town drunks and a few stinking buffalo-runners.

He paused briefly to look around a well-lit, respectable place, the Gray Mule, patronized by the town merchants.

"Looking for someone, Sheriff?" asked Andy from behind the bar.

Toole shook his head and departed silently. He peered into the Cosmopolitan Theater, a variety house popular with the soldiers, and found it dark.

Then he remembered The Mint, a two-story affair a block closer to the Yellowstone and adjacent to the sporting houses. Maybe Sapp had holed up in the sporting houses, but Toole doubted that the madams would want anything to do with him. The Mint, then. Its lower level housed a saloon with gaming tables and a hurdy-gurdy dance floor. Above were rooms, cubicles actually, rented for any purpose whatsoever, with residual odors of sweat, vomit, perfume, and something vaguely sweet and sinister. Home Sweet Home for the likes of Mordecai Sapp.

The weasel of a bartender, bald, dart-eyed, with a scraggle of oily hair snaking over green scalp, peered at Toole sullenly. This place came alive only at night, and usually late at night.

"I'm looking for Sapp," Toole said.

"Never heard of him." The saloonkeep, in a grimy apron, wiped dirt into a glass he pulled from gray water.

"Well, perhaps you've heard of me."

The weasel stared.

"I'm Sapp's doctor. He has a dangerous wound and I'm here to see him. He's up there and I intend to examine him."

"Never heard of him, Sheriff."

Toole sighed. "Neither have I," he muttered.

He edged toward the narrow, steep stairwell in the gloom of the rear, keeping his eye on the weasel.

"Private. Don't let no one up there." The weasel's hands slid below the bar, but Toole had anticipated that. The shining Remington lay in his hand, well aimed.

"I'll tend my patient," Toole said, slipping up the creaking steps into a stinking black hall barely three feet wide.

"Come in, Toole," said Sapp from the far cubicle. The sheriff found him lying on a plank bedstead with a grass-stuffed tick on it, in a room so dark he could barely see. "I did what you said and holed up."

Chapter 4

The wolf growled. Sheriff Toole danced backward into the dim-lit hall. Sapp laughed.

"That's Popskull. Maybe he'll go for your throat, maybe not."

The injured wolf snarled, and Sapp draped a plump hand over its shoulders. The animal settled down.

"I came to see how you're doing."

"No you didn't."

"All right. I came because you're a medical curiosity."

"That's better." It amused Sapp. He prided himself on his realism, and one reality he knew for certain was that no human on earth liked him or cared about him. "Brave the wolf if you want."

Toole edged into the gloom, seeing the creature curled up beside the foul pallet. "I can't see a thing. Is there a candle around or a lamp?"

"People who come in here don't want to see or be seen," Sapp retorted.

"This is scarcely a place to recover your health."

Sapp sighed. "Here," he said, thrusting a yellow candle stub at Toole, one he'd bought from the owner. Toole lit it and held it over Sapp's face. "You don't look dead yet," he said. "How do you feel? Your color's good."

Sapp laughed. "What did you come for?"

Toole glared at him. "Have you headaches? Feel pressure behind your eyes or in your ears? Are the holes draining? Any change in your leg or arm movement?"

34

"What'd you come for?"

"Get up and walk. I want to see you walk. I won't rip those plasters off here; you'd get six new diseases, all of them well deserved."

Sapp chortled. "All right, that's the medicine. Now try the sheriff questions, and then get out." He lay comfortably on his pallet, except for a brutal, throbbing headache.

"They killed all of you. Who did it?"

"They? You confuse me, Sheriff."

"You're hiding from them, whoever they were. Soldiers?"

Sapp fell silent. Toole had found out something with his poking around. "Who's dead? Besides me?" he asked coyly.

"China Belle."

"And . . . ?"

"The rest floated downstream. Who did it, Sapp? You witnessed murder and you can help me. Help yourself."

Sapp laughed nastily. "I never need help."

"I ran into Sergeant Wiltz and some noncoms, looking around there." Toole studied him, waiting for a reaction, but Sapp gave him no satisfaction.

"Who's Wiltz?" he asked.

"How did Wiltz know to come and look around?"

"Who's Wiltz?"

"Is this the way it's going to be, Sapp?"

Sapp smiled sweetly.

"I found bullets. You were killed—shot—in bed. That punk in the lean-to was killed in bed."

"You're a fine detective, Sheriff." The man worried Sapp a bit, poking around like that. No telling what sort of stuff he'd come up with.

Toole sighed. "All right, Sapp, we won't fence anymore. What are your plans?"

"Plans? Plans?"

"Yes, plans. You've been lying here thinking of the future. I want to know what you have in mind. As for your immediate future, I'm telling you as a doctor to stay in Miles, and in bed. In a few days I'll put plates over those holes in your skull, if the wounds look proper. I'll have to do it in my office, with a lot of light and carbolic, and not in this hellhole. Now what are your plans?''

Sapp considered. Plan number one was to live, and that required some attention to what the doctor commanded. Plan number two was to tell this nosy sheriff nothing. Plan number three was to do some traveling to Fort Benton when health permitted, and then only in deepest secrecy. After that . . . He smiled.

''I have no plans at all, Sheriff. Except getting well. I do have a favor to ask, though. That you keep my hiding place secret. And don't tell anyone I'm alive.''

''I already told Wiltz you're alive.''

The news jolted Sapp. ''What did Wiltz say?''

''He laughed. He didn't believe me. Did he do it? Look, Sapp. Some men jumped Hogtown, several of them, probably from the Fort. They dumped all of you in that common grave. Then the storm broke and the rain did its work. I've recovered one and I'll probably find more. I intend to arrest and charge those who did it, and have a hanging. You can help me.''

''No I can't, Sheriff. I was asleep.''

Toole sighed and stood. ''Think about it.''

''I already have, Toole.''

''It's a funny thing. I've been worrying this around in my mind,'' Toole said gently. ''I like to guess, speculate. It's a mental game, I suppose. Here you are, a victim. Parties you know shot you, started to bury you but the deluge' stopped them. I think they shot the rest—finding China Belle's body leads me to that—and every one there died, except yourself.''

Toole eyed him gently. The Irish could do that, Sapp thought, be gentle. It was disconcerting. It reminded him of his gentle parents.

''But your lips are sealed. So I ask myself questions: Why would Mordecai Sapp seal his lips against his tormentors? Lots of possibilities, and I toy with them. Revenge. If you told me who did it, all the powerful processes of law would begin, trials, conviction, or acquittal. But it wouldn't satisfy you. Not for a massacre; not for a bullet through your brain and a cold grave; not for burning all you possess, and killing your people—your slaves. You're a slaver, Sapp. But if you really want revenge, you would do it your own way. Yes. Kill them off one by one, in a way that terrorizes them. You think like that, Sapp. It's plain to me. I'm a little fey, you see.''

Toole was edging too close, and Sapp thought of Popskull. A word to Popskull, who'd been carefully trained. The sheriff waited for a response, but Sapp refused to satisfy him.

"The other thing I came up with, Sapp, is that whoever killed you could do it again." Toole laughed gently. "Kill you twice."

Sapp snorted. "I don't need to hide behind the law."

Toole nodded. "Fight your own battles. In your line, that's understandable. A naked soul. You have no friends and you're on your own. But I'm here to help, man. My badge says I protect people from killers if I can, and I take the badge solemnly, as a man holding office should. Let's talk, Mordecai Sapp."

"Toole, you're a fool Irishman."

Angrily the sheriff vanished into the tobacco-plated hallway. Sapp blew out the candle and slid the derringer clamped in his sweated right hand back under the pad.

Toole tempted him. Enlist the sheriff, set him on Wiltz, Horn, Liggett, Polanc, and the rest. But he'd never resorted to law and didn't like the prospects, such as testifying at a civilian or military trial—the word of Sapp of Hogtown against those soldiers. Toole had a weaker case than he supposed.

If he testified, he'd be a dead man. If those noncoms knew he lived, a witness against them, they'd kill him for sure. That's what made him so itchy about Toole. How the hell did a doctor end up a sheriff?

Sapp settled back under the filthy blanket, one stolen from Fort Keogh, and relaxed in the gloom. He liked the gloom. It rested his eyes, which had been sensitive ever since he'd been shot. The gloom gave him the edge on anyone stepping into the room through the narrow door. It also let him think without distraction, except for an occasional male voice rumbling hollowly from the saloon below.

How much time? Not much. Toole would go out to Fort Keogh, probably tomorrow, and have a chat with Colonel Wade. Wiltz would quickly learn everything that Toole said to the colonel.

Sapp cussed, torn between fleeing Miles and waiting for the plates to be installed in his skull. He had to wait. But he'd move around, though. Here until tomorrow; another dump the next day. Maybe a parlor house if he could buy his way in. Move, so not even Toole would know his whereabouts. . . . But that would be futile. A few noncoms could check every Milestown hidey-hole in an hour.

Head for Benton? Doctors there, too. A hard trip, though, and something cautioned him that he could still croak if he got tired or wet or fevered. A man with two holes in his head required caution.

Leave the country, maybe? No, not that. He'd rebuild Hogtown, and just in time for the bonanza, too. He'd raked in nothing compared to what he'd suck in the next few years. The railroad next year, with armies of gandy dancers spraying dollars. Trail drives from Texas, with payouts to the drovers right here in Miles. Gold galore, far more than the lousy thirteen a month the stupid soldiers got. Rebuild, then. Buy some more dollies. Dumb young dollies off the immigrant boats. A chinee and a mulatto for spice. A little opium, a little hash for the heavy spenders. Some new gunmen to enforce the rules. Order more redeye and popskull. Get more tables and games up from Denver City. Get rich in a few more years and then get out of this miserable prairie hole. San Francisco . . .

One little hitch, though. Sergeant Major Vernon Wiltz. And a few others who were in on it, who'd kill him again for keeps if they discovered he lived.

A trial, ha! That papist, Irish, old-world idiot Toole hadn't figured out the frontier, for sure. Did that bonehead think the army would stand still for that? They'd maybe rap Wiltz's knuckles lightly and free him. No. Only one way lay open: Kill them off, every noncom, until he could open Hogtown again without fear.

Sapp pondered events. He had a way of putting himself in the shoes of others. He put himself in Wiltz's boots and swiftly understood that the sergeant would murder the sheriff if he had to, if Toole probed too close to the truth. He put himself in Toole's office and felt Toole's passion for bringing the killers to justice. And more. Toole had doctored those dollies and cared something for them. Sapp had figured that out long ago, when Toole had hovered in their cribs, mostly listening to the dumb girls wail while he treated their diseases with salves of mercury and arsenic. That had suited Sapp fine: Dead dollies were no use to him. So Toole might be driven by something else, some sentimental, personal thing. . . .

Fascinating, thought Sapp. Maybe he could play a few marked cards or arrange the shuffle. But how? He had no answers at the moment. He eased lower into his nest, enjoying the summer heat and the dive's darkness, feeling secure in his hidey-hole. Soon the night's debauch would begin below, and he'd have to wait alertly with derringer in hand as dark bodies slid by, headed for other little pestholes along the corridor.

He'd get out of this one soon, when he had enough money. He intended to retire at forty-five, four years hence. Rich. A lot richer than his parents in Indiana, who still clung to the communal life in New Harmony, even after the cooperative colony of Robert Owen had collapsed. Lofty-minded and dirt-poor, that's how his father lived, giving away whatever he raised so that loafers could gobble it and getting nothing but sweet smiles in return. The old man hoed and plowed and milked and toted and ground away his life for the sake of a lofty system of robbery that had a polite name. Mordecai had understood the folly of it by age nine, after working his young fingers to bone to feed those parasites. By age eleven he knew he'd leave the colony and get rich. By age thirteen he was on his own, practicing his own species of enterprise—stealing on the levee of St. Louis—until he got together enough to begin his true calling. And loathing his stupid parents.

Santiago Toole woke up thrashing and choking, wanting air. He bolted upright in bed, lungs sucking, heart howling. The ivory light of a gibbous moon pierced through the wavery glass of his window, throwing ghostly light on his sheet, on Mimi beside him. Her eyes caught his.

"Santiago . . ."

"Bad dream," he muttered, his terror subsiding in the quiet.

She sat up languorously, her back to the walnut headboard, her small breasts honeyed by the moonlight.

"Tell me about it, Santo." A gentle hand caught his chest, splaying curly chest hair under it.

"I can't." He couldn't because he'd relived that killer punch, felt it strike and paralyze him, felt himself struggle for air with lungs that wouldn't work.

"What happened today? When someone hurt you."

"A hard punch that knocked the breath out of me."

"More than that. It almost killed you. I heard you talk in your sleep."

He didn't reply at first, and her caress told him he didn't need to.

"Wiltz did it. The sergeant major at the fort. There was a message in it, if I lived."

"Stay away," she whispered. "But you won't stay away, and now you wake up with nightmares."

Sometimes she understands me all too well, he thought. Lucky at love sometimes means no secrets. He was lucky at love, and she fathomed him deeper than he fathomed himself.

"I have a duty to my office."

She said nothing.

He would have to ride to the Fort and talk with Colonel Orville Prescott Wade. He'd have to ask for an investigation. Reveal his suspicions. Tell Wade that he was investigating and might bring civilian charges. And outside the door that killer Wiltz would be listening at his desk. That thought made his skin prickle and his belly sweat. Running that gauntlet to and from Wade's office would be as much as he could cope with. Maybe more. The terror of that blow suffused him, and he wondered if he could do it; make himself march over there, announce himself to Wade's adjutant or Wiltz—one or the other—and get on with it, in spite of Wiltz's murderous warning. Suicide. Going to Fort Keogh would be suicide.

"You're afraid," Mimi said.

"More than I've ever been in my life."

"But you'll do it anyway."

She understood and didn't beg him not to, as other women might have. Somehow in the morning he would make his legs work and proceed spastically to discuss matters with the colonel, and probably die for it. He yearned for a way out and found none. Run his own investigation, never tell the army, get warrants when he got his evidence together . . . but without the army he wouldn't get much evidence together. He had one bullet-pierced corpse of a Chinese harlot no one cared about; another hidden victim of attempted murder who was not talking; and a few mashed, spent bullets. Plus a hole that had been a grave. Not much.

"Tell me," she said.

"I need the army's help. But if I ask for it, I think Wiltz or one of his noncoms will try to kill me, somehow."

"You don't have to go so soon. Maybe the man you helped will talk about it."

"Mimi, what do you know about him?" he asked sharply.

"Only what I heard. He came at dawn and you helped him."

Holy Mary, he thought, Mimi's life is in danger, too, from the simple innocent knowledge that a man—Sapp—came to my door needing a doctor.

"Forget that it happened."

"You have secrets from me?"

"Yes, Mimi."

He felt her hand pause in its gentle rounds over his shoulders and chest and then resume its caresses.

"It's the first time. Is there something between us?"

"Your safety."

"I've always trusted you."

"Mimi . . . a man like Wiltz could wring anything from you."

"Then he'd find out what I do know—that you helped a man at dawn."

"Mimi . . . Sergeant Wiltz is the most dangerous man I've ever met. A killer. Whatever you do, stay out of his sight now."

"You love me," she replied.

"He might come here, Mimi."

A breeze billowed the lace curtains at his window, its eddying air drying the nightmare sweat on his body. He drifted fitfully into oblivion again, feeling her settle beside him and arch herself close to him. Dear Mimi.

In the soft June morning he took her counsel and decided to wait a day. This one he'd devote to searching the river banks by riding horseback ten or fifteen miles east. Several bullet-riddled bodies would command more attention from Wade and the officers at Keogh than just one, a poor Chinese girl.

He saddled his bay and stopped at Tobias's shop to borrow a spare horse. Tobias's horses would not panic under the sort of load Toole proposed to tie to their backs.

"Help yourself," the ruddy man said. "I got three: Heaven, Hell, and Purgatory. You're a papist, so take Purgatory, the gray."

Toole laughed.

"See here. I been busy, Sheriff." The cabinetmaker led Toole into a small parlor used for the mortuary business. A slim box of some hardwood rested on sawhorses there, beneath two bouquets of black-eyed susans exploding in brass and canary and peach colors in the early-morning sun.

"Some layout for a chinee," he said proudly.

It annoyed Toole. "Sylvane. That girl never had any choice. She'd been sold—literally sold—by her desperate mother to a tong lord. He sold her again to a white man. She was sold two more times until Sapp bought her. Sylvane, do you know how they keep those creatures? No clothes. Not a stitch to escape with. Pump opium into them until they're addicted. Always the menace of a killer hovering around. Not to mention a whip. And an occasional beating just for lessons. Sylvane, if you have an ounce of goodness in your small mean heart, pity her."

"Yeah, I do, but Toole, she was a yellow heathen, not a good Christian woman. Maybe that's the good Lord's way of dealing with the yellow heathen. . . ."

"You're calling God a slaver and whoremonger!" Toole roared.

Tobias subsided at once.

"Let's bury her when I get back. Sometime this afternoon. I'll be here, and Mimi. And you'll have a proper hole dug."

"I'll have to start a chinee corner in the yard."

lared at him and stalked back to Tobias's barn to gray. Angrily he led the gray down the river-bank path eastward from Milestown, into a fresh, glowing morning. The big sky arched azure overhead, its air clear and dry. Prairie steppes lay like shelves, mounting upward in lemon folds pierced occasionally by streaks of coral and russet. He didn't expect to find anything. The angry green river boiled with mountain runoff, a frothy gray, bubbling torrent that would rip floating human bodies off of snags and tumble them down to the great Missouri, far to the northeast. And yet I'll try, he thought stubbornly. No good sheriff could do less.

He had never dreamed of being a sheriff. That had come to him by accident when the town fathers couldn't find a proper man. He'd made barely two hundred cash dollars at medicine that year, give or take a few chickens and an old saddle. He had accepted—temporarily, of course—and discovered he had a knack for it.

All morning he rode, probing out onto necks of land when the trail veered from them, studying brush and snags, dismounting once to hop and slide out on a pile of cottonwood trunks and river debris. And finding nothing. Around noon, when the sun was roasting him and scorching through his black vest, he turned back, defeated.

Chapter 5

Santiago wished he hadn't brought Mimi. A mob, mostly female, had collected around Tobias's shop, waiting for the show to begin. Word of China Belle's funeral had certainly been bandied from one end of Milestown to the other. And of course some had seen China Belle resting in state, with those masses of yellow daisies upon her casket.

These were the parlorhouse girls, come to bury one of their own. Almost one of their own, for a great gulf ran between these free harlots and the little Chinese slave from a hellhole up the river. He studied them quietly, not exactly liking what he saw. Some wore severe and proper clothing, high-necked, somber summer dresses that hid all traces of their trade, other than what could be read in their faces. Others flaunted it, wearing gaudy things that exposed acres of bosom and white arms and supplied diaphanous glimpses of limb and ankle. Twelve ladies of the trade, he counted, and two madams, bejeweled and corseted in somber, rich rags.

"You gonna bury her, Sheriff?" asked one he knew as Juney, who wore a gauzy red thing so provocative she shouldn't have been on the street. He could see her limbs through it.

"I'll do my best."

"You mind our coming or are you gonna lecture us? We don't want no Bible lectures."

"China Belle was my patient and my friend," he retorted sharply.

"We came because no one else would."

A harlot's funeral, then. He pulled Mimi to him, glad of her prim white dress that lent dignity to this event. Glad of his own black frock coat and vest and boiled white collar and pin-striped pants, which would do well enough for a doctor and sheriff playing the role of divine. He knew them all, having doctored them many times for nameless diseases of sinning flesh. Few men. Neither the town's merchants and their ladies, nor the sporting types who used and abused creatures like these. Several yellow curs, all barking, and a few boys, gaping and elbowing each other and grinning stupidly at the whores.

"Hey, Sheriff!" cried one. "You gonna have a chinee whore funeral? Firecrackers and joss sticks and all that?"

Santiago paused before the carrot-topped lad. "No, son. Prayers and quiet."

"For a heathen?"

"For one of God's children. You go home now. This isn't for you. None of you boys."

The sharpness of his voice had its effect, and the curious children drew back. He slipped his hand in Mimi's and entered Tobias's clapboarded white establishment. The cabinetmaker, now attired in swallowtail coat and boiled shirt and bow tie, stood ready.

"I'm ready, Sheriff. Got old Hell harnessed up, and we'll head up the hill."

"Not Hell, Mr. Tobias. Heaven. Harness Heaven. The dappled white."

"But Sheriff, she's not—"

"Heaven, Tobias, or you won't get paid."

"Purgatory?"

"Heaven, Sylvane."

Grumbling, the man slid out back, while Santiago and Mimi stood quietly before the shining casket.

"I'm glad you cared about her," she said softly. "It must be terrible to die alone. No one caring. *Mon Dieu,* terrible."

Mimi looked particularly Indian in the light of the twin candles, and particularly beautiful. Her body seemed more Assiniboin than French, but her mind, schooled downriver, seemed more French than Indian.

"That reminds me, Mimi. Later I want to ask you something."

Tobias, looking slightly sweated in the June heat, reappeared, and together they lifted the light burden and carried it through the door and out to Tobias's wagon. He had no proper hearse; none existed in this raw frontier settlement. But his spring wagon, draped in black bunting, served the purpose. Tobias clambered into the seat and flicked his lines, and Heaven hunkered into her harness and drew the wagon out into the broad avenue. There the strange procession began: Santiago and Mimi immediately behind the wagon with the doxies of Miles following, while lounging males smirked from covered porches and storefront benches.

It occurred to Santiago that he didn't even know her real name. Only China Belle, a thing made up by one or another of her masters. No name. He wondered what he'd say. What could a Catholic lawman say about a Chinese harlot, to an audience of bawds? Talk of slavery and a hard lot in life? These sashaying ladies behind him knew all about that. They ranked many notches up the scale from the wretched denizens of Hogtown, free rather than slave, able to keep some of their earnings rather than losing every last penny of it. And yet, every one of them knew how close she was to China Belle, and that for some of those no longer young and fresh and blooming some Hogtown or Hog ranch loomed months away. . . .

No, he'd not talk of slavery. A zephyr whipped Mimi's white skirts, revealing her long, lovely form, and for a moment Santiago forgot his solemn purposes here and watched her, entranced. She did that to him. The wagon rattled ahead through the somber, sunny afternoon. Heaven lifted her tail, and then lowered her tail delicately. Santiago and Mimi skirted the green piles, and the procession divided behind them. From the walks someone smirked, and a sideways glance revealed the blue blouse of a soldier, lounging against a porch post. Santiago recoiled slightly, wished he had armed himself in some way, or at least pinned on his lapel the steel circlet that was his badge of office and honor. He glanced again, and spotted a corporal's hashmarks, even as the smirker lollygagged along behind the procession.

So, news has reached the fort, he thought. News did that in a tiny, rough town squatting defiantly in a vast wilderness. The two-rut road hairpinned up the southerly bluffs of the river, toward the high ground that lay at the confluence of the Tongue and Yellowstone, up to a windswept small plot there, zealously sliced into sections: Catholic, Protestant, Masons, whores, a potter's field for vagrants and unknown . . . and now in a far exotic corner, a shallow trench for a Chinese, who didn't rate even a harlot's berth here.

Mr. Tobias drove the rattling wagon serenely toward its isolated destination, and then stopped. Except for the whip of relentless prairie wind, no sound arose here. The bawds and strumpets gathered quietly in a circle around the shallow hole chipped out of resisting yellow gumbo. They were all waiting for him, he knew. Waiting to see what the Irish sheriff, rather new to these dry lonely lands, would say. Ready to condemn, he thought. Tobias pulled a large kerchief from his pocket and honked his nose, looking faintly amused. A story to tell the boys down the slope over a beer later on.

Suddenly Santiago Toole felt at a loss. He glanced helplessly at Mimi, who smiled quietly. Still not knowing, he rounded the trench to stand at its head, facing these solemn ladies, whose every mole and birthmark beneath the layers of gauzy, gaudy cloth were all too familiar to him.

"Does anyone know her real name?" he asked.

No one did.

"Then we'll bury her as China Belle, and remember her that way."

That seemed agreeable to the silent women.

"I've not come to bury a heathen and an outcast, but one of Our Lord's own," he began, searching desperately for words. "If her spirit can see you now—and I think she can—I know she must be glad that you are here to say good-bye and to remember her. It is good of you to come. We all hope that when our own time comes, someone will be there to say good-bye. In life, no one remembered her, or cared. From her girlhood, China Belle was a slave and forbidden to follow her own will."

He peered sharply into these faces, these silent doxies, and thought he perceived a subtle relaxation coming over them.

"She struggled to escape her bonds, her slavery to opium, her poverty, her imprisonment, her diseases. She had no place to escape to, no place to go, no living to earn once she broke free. In the end, the hell she lived with seemed less frightening than the hell she'd face as a Chinese girl out in the world. I failed to help her. She suffered her days in a place as foul as any on earth, and run by mortals as wicked as any, and patronized''—he spotted that blue blouse now out at the edge of the women—''patronized by soldiers as uncaring and hellish as the owner of that place.''

It pleased him, his words reaching that smirky corporal there. That seemed enough. He didn't want to draw this thing out. He ruffed through the pages of a small Bible he carried, thinking not of prayer but of something else. He found the text he'd marked.

"Let this be our good-bye to China Belle," he said.

"Blessed are the poor in spirit, for theirs is the Kingdom of Heaven.

"Blessed are those who mourn, for they shall be comforted.

"Blessed are the meek, for they shall inherit the earth.

"Blessed are those who hunger and thirst for righteousness, for they shall be satisfied.

"Blessed are the merciful, for they shall obtain mercy."

This he directed toward the two males present, the corporal and Sylvane Tobias. He read the rest of the Beatitudes, closed his Bible, and recited the Lord's Prayer, pausing while the Protestants added their Gloria to it, and then the silence folded home.

"Corporal," he said. "Lend a hand."

The ruddy man stared and then approached, reluctantly, and the three of them, Tobias, Toole, and the corporal, lifted the small wooden box and settled it into the gashed breast of the earth. Tobias shoveled until the mustard clay lay heaped over the grave. Mimi picked up the two great bouquets and settled them gently on the mounded, raw earth, and it was done.

Some of the bawds paused solemnly there, one wept, and then they all walked on down the grassy windswept slope, with its views of the Fort in the distance, Milestown, the Tongue, and the Yellowstone. And last, even after Tobias's wagon had rattled along ahead, Santiago Toole and Mimi walked quietly home.

*   *   *

Fear writhed in Santiago like a chained monster threatening to break its bonds. More than fear, he knew. Hysteria. He stood at the edge, wrestling with Duty. He didn't have to ride to Fort Keogh; he could sheriff and doctor just as well staying close to Miles. But some iron imperative made him go, even though the memory of that murderous punch and the threat carried with it howled in him, made him sweat, even brought him echoes of the pain and terror he'd experienced when his body quit working.

Holy Mary, why didn't he just resign and move elsewhere? Was there no power in the universe, even the intercession of saints, that might make this journey easier? Nothing helped him; not prayer, not a mental review of all that medicine had to say about fear and hysteria, not positive thinking. In the end, as he saddled his bay, optimism helped. The world smiled on the audacious. A determined man might enlist the hidden powers of the world. In this case, perhaps, officers who cared about murder done by their men. Maybe even Wiltz—if he was innocent—might see the light and begin an inquiry intended to root out the evil coiled there in the barracks of Keogh. And if worse came to worse, the big black Remington heavy on his hip might speak with its own authority.

He rode tautly westward from Miles, the horse sensing his uneasiness and spooky beneath him as its hooves drummed the Tongue River bridge. A golden morning, but he scarcely knew it, so busy was he rehearsing his message. He hoped the star pinned to his black vest might convey its own power, but he doubted it. What respect had the army for a sheriff's badge? He hoped his words might convey moral power, but the army wasn't in the morals business—its power lay in the bores of guns.

The Fort lay well back from the Yellowstone, a prim oblong of white clapboard and dun brick in debauched wilderness. It seemed to see everything, its cyclops eye observing the passage of red ants and soaring crows. Toole had often felt that to ride to Fort Keogh was to close in on the charged bores of a thousand explosive arms, though in fact little of that was visible this somnolent morning. Fort Keogh had come a long way from the crude cantonment of log and canvas erected in the autumn of 1876, in the wake of the Little Big Horn a little to the south. Those huts of misery and frostbite had yielded to army comfort, six million pounds of wood and furnishings shipped piecemeal upriver from distant Leavenworth and other points.

Sheriff Toole rode straight into the cyclops eye, past blue-clad guards, past enlisted men's barracks that stared dourly across a dusty parade toward officers' quarters on the far side. He steered toward the centermost of the officers' quarters, a wooden structure before which a flag on a staff flapped in the vicious prairie breezes. Headquarters for Nelson Miles's Fifth Infantry, Department of Dakota, as well as home for Major and Brevet Colonel Orville Prescott Wade, commander of walk-a-heap infantry that bragged it could walk down any Indian village in four months. He tied his bay at the hitchrail and mounted ten wooden stairs to a small portico and a yellow-varnished door. He paused there to still his soul, unclench his jaw, and stretch his balled fists.

Holy Mary, he thought, will life always be so hard? He felt the mounting hysteria in him, and pushed open the door to enter a barren wooden room with two battered desks, one for the absent adjutant, the other for the sergeant major.

Who looked up and grinned malevolently.

"A slow learner," said Sergeant Wiltz.

"I've come to see Colonel Wade."

"About?"

"Hogtown."

"Ah, Hogtown! And what will you tell the colonel?"

"I'm sure he will share it with you, Sergeant."

"Ah, Hogtown. Which doesn't exist, does it, Sheriff? So there is nothing to tell the colonel?"

Every instinct in Santiago Toole howled at him to turn and leave. Instead he heard himself say, "There's been murder, Sergeant."

Wiltz said nothing, his feral eyes gazing at the slender sheriff, his bullet head, bull neck, and massive torso radiating menace and amusement, as if he were examining some cowering boy recruit. Then he grinned suddenly. "Why, murder. Of enlisted men, perhaps? A terrible thing."

"Colonel Wade, please."

"One never knows who will get it next, does one, Sheriff?"

The sergeant major stood suddenly, looming like some malevolent dinosaur, and vanished through the brown-painted door behind him.

The plank-walled room ticked like a clock.

The door opened suddenly, howling on its hinges, yanked by some unimaginable force, and Wiltz emerged, a blue hulk in a mustard-colored, wainscoted room.

"Why, step right in, Sheriff. The colonel loves a good murder or two."

He loomed in the doorway, half blocking it with his own massive body, forcing Toole to ease by, close, so close, close enough for that murderous uppercut that would end him. Toole swallowed down the terror in his throat and slid by, feeling the brush of Toole's belly. He found himself in Wade's guidon-decked inner sanctum.

Dizzy suddenly, dizzy from gulped-down hysteria and a racing pulse.

"Sheriff Toole . . . are you well?"

Wade rose from behind his desk, peering owlishly at Toole from behind round gold-rimmed spectacles. An oddly pale man for a frontier officer, with liver spots marching over his ivory scalp. Then the colonel settled back in his swivel chair.

Toole relaxed slightly.

"Sergeant major says you have something to tell us about Hogtown . . . ? Toole, are you all right?"

"I am," he said, recovering his wits. He turned slightly. Wiltz had left the door wide open and would hear every word.

"Hogtown, you know, is off your reservation and under civil jurisdiction. My jurisdiction."

"All hogtowns, all hog ranches, all hogfarms are," said Wade acidly. "Yours burned. How nice."

"It was burned," Toole continued doggedly. "And I believe its inmates were murdered."

"Yes, yes, you buried one slut yesterday. Fished from the river. Very kind of you. Too kind."

"I imagine Sergeant Wiltz told you."

"Why yes, he keeps me well informed of all the doings in Milestown. Have you other evidence? More bodies?"

"Some evidence. Enough to know that the male inmates were shot in bed simultaneously and the women killed later. That the thing had been systematic, planned, and executed according to a well-conceived idea. By several assailants, probably five or six."

Wade steepled and unsteepled his white fingers.

"I'd like your assistance. Everything points to the Fort. This was no crime of passion, no work of a loner, and not the work of a stray buffalo-runner gone mad. It was the work of organized killers who knew what they were doing."

"One body and you accuse the army of a massacre?"

"I'd like a thorough investigation. That or a chance to question your men myself."

"Murder, yes. I don't approve of murder. Even though these diseased vermin deserved it. You know, Sheriff, this whole thing pleases me. We'll clear out our hospital wards. I expect we'll see fewer deserters. And materiel—my goodness gracious, Toole, you have no idea how much—"

"I have a good idea," Toole said.

"I'm puzzled, Sheriff. You say you have evidence. Now I don't want to start some wild goose chase. . . . You'd better tell us what you know. In fact, if you withhold information, I'm afraid we'll have to—hold you. This is army territory, you know. You and Miles exist only because we're keeping the Sioux and Cheyenne under control. What's your evidence, Toole?"

"I don't think the territorial government would take it kindly if the army impeded or thwarted a sheriff's murder investigation," Toole said mildly.

Wade snorted. "How far away is Helena, Sheriff?"

"A little farther than regimental headquarters at Fort Shaw, Colonel. I can report to either."

Wade frowned. Toole wondered if he'd been wise to meet a threat with a threat.

Wade drummed his fingers on the varnish of his desk. "What evidence, Toole? I haven't a thing to go on. If you want an army inquiry, you'd better supply some reasonable grounds for it. I'll tell you frankly, I'm delighted that hellhole burned down,and I'm not inclined to look very closely at it.''

Santiago Toole was facing his Rubicon. Retreat now to safety; or tell what he'd found out, and face whatever came. He walked gently to the door behind him and closed it, while Wade watched. Then he edged close to Wade's desk and leaned over it.

"Colonel, my prime suspect is your man here, Wiltz. Wiltz and some others. There was a witness.''

Chapter 6

Colonel Wade's lips flapped like a bottom-feeding carp's.

"A witness? This person saw my men commit murder?"

"I believe he saw just that."

"Who is he?"

"Confidential, for now."

"Well, Sheriff, where is he? Who's he talked to?"

Toole shook his head.

"If you have the goods why do you need me—us—an army investigation?" A thought came to him, and he smiled. "I think this witness isn't very credible—his word against the word of our good men here. Is that it? One of those swine over there trying to wreck the army. You're a sucker, Sheriff."

Toole shook his head again, smiling faintly. He did not intend to give anything away just yet. Not until he got Sapp's story from him.

"Bull. It's all bull. A witness you won't name. I think you're fishing, Sheriff. You find a body and Hogtown burnt down and you want us to snoop around among our men. . . ."

Toole nodded. "That's what I want, Colonel. I'd like an officer to question them all, see who drew fresh revolver rounds yesterday, find out where they were that night, probe for motives."

"Fresh revolver rounds? You're saying that the sergeant—"

Toole put a finger to his lips. "Secret. I've collected a few spent bullets that didn't melt. All the same caliber. All from here, I believe. Evidence, Colonel. May I have your confidential cooperation?"

Wade eased back into his chair, his gaze darting fearfully toward the closed door. Toole sensed dread in the man, and understood it all too well. Wade looked and acted trapped.

"No. No, Toole. We'll handle this matter ourselves and I want you to let it be. It's our kettle of fish."

Santiago Toole caught Wade's eye and read the hostility in it. "I won't ask again, Colonel. But I'll say a few things and you'll bloody well listen. I'm hunting down those killers. Maybe enlisted men, but probably your noncoms. Your noncoms are free to slip out at night. They've the skills to perform a little massacre they think needs doing."

The colonel grinned malevolently.

Toole stabbed a finger at him. "If I nail this down, I won't come to you with it. I'm going to talk to people at regimental headquarters. And civilian authorities. Then where will you be—having refused to cooperate in a murder investigation?"

"But . . . Toole." The colonel hunted for words, as if addressing a small, dull child. "These were crooks and bawds, opium-eaters, thieves of government property, heathen. . . ."

"Mortals, Colonel."

"Don't point fingers, Toole. You think you can just go off shredding the command here, go your own way. . . . I should clap you in irons. By God, I'll clap you in irons, Toole, unless you lay off. Now. Right now. Try me, Toole. See how safe you are off the military reservation. I'll throw you in our guardhouse so fast you won't know what hit you. You think that badge will protect you? I can talk too, you know. I'll have reasons. I always have reasons. And when I'm done you'll never see daylight again. You're dealing with the United States Infantry, Sheriff. . . . And I'll tell you something else: Milestown' is a small place. If you've really got a witness stashed over there, we'll find him inside of an hour. Any hour."

Wade's lips compressed into a thin line. Toole read the rage building in the commanding officer and stood solidly.

Colonel Wade erupted from his chair. "I'll decide what I want to do later, Sheriff," he said in a voice elaborately calm.

A nod dismissed him, and Santiago saw no reason to press further. He'd only made another enemy, a powerful one who could work his will on any civilian, even one in authority. Toole kicked himself mentally for his intransigence, for making enemies when he needed allies, for letting his anger, his indignation rule his common sense. And now he faced the gauntlet again.

With sweated palms he twisted the knob and opened the door. It didn't howl on its hinges, the way it had in Wiltz's hands. Wiltz leaned back in his chair, smirking faintly, reading something. An ancient, tattered magazine, *Godey's Lady's Book* in fact.

"I like to learn about women. Good night, Sheriff," he said as Toole slid past, his hand hovering close to his Remington. He'd kill Wiltz before he'd let the sergeant get in close again. But the sergeant stayed rooted to his chair, and Toole, cold-handed and sweated, slipped out into the shadow of the portico, blinking his eyes at the harsh morning sun.

Good night, the sergeant major had said. Santiago found in that a whole red diagram of his future. He mounted his bay clumsily and wheeled away, feeling a thousand bores aimed at his back. It was all he could do to stick to a slow trot.

He rode toward Milestown feeling too small for his office, wondering whether to turn in his badge. They'd turned the tables on him, threatened to hunt him down, jail him, if he kept on poking into the Hogtown affair. Wiltz might kill him. Wade would settle for ruining him somehow. If he quit would he be a coward, hating himself? He could practice medicine, forget the lawing, forget that this had happened, just go on setting broken limbs, spraying wounds with carbolic, bandaging cuts, spooning out laudanum to the suffering, quinine for the ague, assafetida, belladonna, foxglove and ipecac, growing into fusty, silver-haired old age loved and trusted by all—except himself. For as long as he peered into his looking glass when he put the straightedge to his jaws, he'd see a gently bred man who hadn't measured up when the rough yardsticks of this new land took his height.

He hitched the bay at a rail before The Mint, down below the rest of the town. The place sagged and looked abused, though it had been built only a year before. He found the door locked—too early—but spotted the bartender sucking coffee at a table in the dim light at the rear. He rattled the door. The barkeep dourly ignored him.

"Open up," he snapped. "Or I'll bust it open."

Indolently the man approached, and Toole heard a hasp sliding, and the door creak.

"Sheriff?" the man asked.

Toole rammed the door, spilling the man behind it, and trotted toward the gloomy little stair at the rear. Ancient dried tobacco assaulted him, along with other acrid and foul odors, including urine, beer, and something sweet. He drummed up the hollow stairwell, erupting into the dank corridor, and plunged into Sapp's room. Nothing. He waited for his eyes to adjust. No one. One by one, he ripped the other flimsy doors open, peering into each cubicle. A woozy naked drunk in one. Nothing in the others. He clattered down the stairs, making a racket, and found the barkeep back at his coffee.

"Where's Sapp?"

The man shrugged.

"I told you before, I'm his doctor. He needs constant medical attention."

"So who cares?"

A good question, Toole thought. No one on earth cared about Sapp. "I think you have ways of reaching him. Tell him I want to see him tonight. In my office. After dark. And to watch out."

The man yawned.

"Tell him—or I'll lean on this place so bad you'll close up."

The man smirked gently. "That's what I like about dainty Irish sheriffs," he said. "Big mouths, little guts."

Toole stalked out, wanting sun and clean air.

Mimi had never seen him in such a state. He'd stormed in at mid-morning, looking pale and crazed, as though a thousand wolves were snapping at his heels. He banged into his study, and she heard the chatter of the rolltop desk, and then silence. She started a fire for tea, though she hated to heat the stove on a hot summer day. Still, tea calmed him down. Tea revived Britons and Irishmen. She peered into his study and saw him writing fiercely, jabbing his steel-nib pen into the pot and scraping out the letters, blotting and muttering every few words. Once he glared up at her, as if to say she'd trespassed.

Then he hunted up a ball-peen hammer and disappeared into the backyard, where the buggy and spring wagon sagged in the sun. There he began hammering and mumbling to himself, hammering on something yellow, using the iron tire of the wagon as a kind of anvil. She took his tea to him there, and found him mauling an innocent gold eagle, spreading the malleable gold outward and thinning its edges almost to razor sharpness, constantly measuring his work with a small ruler.

She watched silently, less curious about this strange labor of his than about the volcanic heat radiating out of him. Her father, old Marceau, had once said the French have mad passions and cold minds, while the Assiniboin have cold passions and mad minds. Her Assiniboin mother retorted that all whites were crazy. Looking at Toole, she thought maybe her mother had it right.

"Here's tea," she said.

He paused, stared at her, and returned to his labor. "Later," he muttered.

She watched him while the tea grew cold, watched him tap and file and measure and compare the measurements to some figures on a scrap of paper. He peered at both golden wafers critically and slipped them into his pocket.

He seemed to discover her there and his eyes grew hot and tender.

"Mimi," he said hoarsely, taking her into his arms. "Mimi. I told you I had a question to ask. Will you marry me?"

She gasped. "Santo!"

They'd lived together for two years as man and wife, not caring if anyone knew. But no one knew.

He pushed apart so he could peer soulfully into her brown eyes. "Mimi. If anything should happen to me, you'd not be protected, not inherit. You'd be cast out. This isn't right."

She gawked at him, astounded by this turn of events. "But Santo. I don't want to get married. And besides, where's the priest?"

"When one comes—we'll have one. But we can go to the

justice now. That would make it proper. We must be proper, Mimi!''

''No, Santo. If we marry you'll grow tired of me and not—'' She smiled at him. ''I'm half-Assiniboin. I don't want to stay all the time in your world. I think sometime I will find a man among my mother's people. I have two bloods, and I like my other one too. Ah, oh Santo. You're unhappy.''

''Mimi, we must do it. It'd be right. So little separates you from those—''

''Parlorhouse ladies? I'm one of those, Santiago?''

''No, no, no, Mimi. Holy Mary, is nothing sacred anymore, the sacrament of matrimony, the bonds, the vows to live side by side forever?''

Something in her melted. ''Oh, Santiago, it's sweet of you. But I'm French. And Indian. A breed. Two bloods at war in me. And you know how the white ladies treat—''

''I know and I hate it.''

''But you're sweet to ask. Don't you want your tea?''

He looked hurt. ''Mimi, it wasn't a joke. It was the best way I knew to express my love for you.''

She tugged at him. ''Come inside, Santiago, and tell me what's wrong. What happened at Fort Keogh this morning? Why are you writing things? You've seen a ghost.''

She dragged it out of him in the kitchen, at least some of it; his treatment at Keogh, the threats of bodily harm, the colonel's skepticism and hostility, his hopes of bringing those who murdered Hogtown's inmates to justice.

''I wasn't bred for this, Mimi. These frontier Americans are a harder breed than I can deal with, tougher and meaner and more brutal than any in Europe. Better and worse, in larger doses, than any. . . . And I'm not one. I'm just a sentimental man with a little flame of justice burning in me, and not the fists and courage to do anything with it.''

''Santiago Toole, you're the strongest man I know. Fists don't solve everything. Guns don't either. But your courage can, and your goodness can.''

''I'm no more virtuous than anyone else.''

''Less virtuous,'' she said. She laughed and hugged him. ''I've written two things. One is a will giving you everything I possess. The other is an account of this case so far, which I want you to deliver to the territorial governor if anything happens to me. They're stashed in my desk in a back corner, out of the way.''

''We'll see,'' she said.

''But Mimi—I want you. . . .''

''What were you doing with the gold?''

''Corks. Those are medical versions of corks. We'll have a night visitor, I believe. And I will install the corks.'' At last he laughed a little.

The rap on the rear door came at eleven well after she'd gone to bed. She didn't intend to miss whatever this would be for anything, so she whirled out of the sheets, slipped chemise and petticoat on, pulled her summery green calico over her head and settled it on her body.

She burst into his office and found it glowing golden with lamplight. Some whale of a man sat in the creaking rocker, pushed so far back that he stared at the ceiling, while Santiago doctored the man's head. She gaped, seeing a filthy purple coat with black velvet collar, grimy broadcloth pants, dirty hightops.

''No Mimi! Not here! Not now!''

''But Santo . . .''

The man jerked his head up and gazed at her through oily eyes encased in layered fat. He snorted, and then wheezed.

''You're not fit to look at her. Not fit to be in the same room with her, Sapp.'' Santiago dabbed at the man's scalp with something pungent. ''Mimi—please leave.''

''I won't,'' she retorted.

''Then help me. Hold the rocker back so he faces up.''

She walked to the chair and found herself gaping into a hole in the man's skull, with slippery gray brain pulsing at its base. Santiago had cleaned away the mess around it until clean bone showed. Deftly he sliced scalp free of the bone around the hole and then pulled one of the flattened gold pieces from a tumbler of carbolic. She realized Santiago was patching the man's skull.

''Sapp, I'm going to spray your brains with carbolic. I haven't the faintest idea what that'll do. Kill you I hope. Or maybe the acid will eat away your sins. Consider it medical communion.''

Sapp guffawed.

He squirted the carbolic in mist form into the open wound while Mimi held the man's greasy head, suspecting that if she dug into that filthy hair she'd find lice.

Then Santiago gently slipped the golden wafer over the hole, pulling scalp over it around the edges until it was anchored in place. He knotted Sapp's own hair over the plate to pin it down for a while, until it grew out.

"There. That's the only clean thing about you.''

"What's carbolic do?''

"Antiseptic. It kills germs, bacteria.''

"Like little spiders?''

"No, microscopic. Too small for the eye. That's how we control infection now. I took my degree in Scotland and saw Joseph Lister himself doing it. He figured it out—took some ideas of Pasteur's. . . . Mimi, hold him lower.''

She pushed the rockers down with her foot, and Santiago began working on the other hole, above the man's ear.

"Two holes. Was he shot through the head, Santo?''

Toole muttered.

"Got me at Hogtown. Buried me alive,'' Sapp boasted.

"Hogtown,'' Mimi repeated faintly, sudden loathing permeating her. Santiago glared at her.

"Who got you, Sapp? Who buried you?''

"Dammit, I go to a doctor and get a sheriff.''

"I need to know,'' Santiago said, jabbing his carbolic-soaked cotton hard around the side wound.

"Ow, you bastard sawbones.''

"Mimi, this is not for you.''

She glared back at him, defying him to order her out.

"Sapp,'' he said, dabbing at the exposed hole, "you're a medical impossibility. You're dead. So tell me who killed you. I've figured some of it out. Several of them jumped the men, shot you in your beds. I found some bullets. Then they herded the women somewhere and shot them. Who, Sapp? Enlisted men? Noncoms? I don't suppose they were officers but I'll consider that, too.''

Sapp guffawed, a booming snarl that erupted from the belly.

"I talked with Colonel Wade. He's not helpful. In fact, he's protecting whoever did it. So it's up to you, Sapp. Tell me and I'll work on it. You name them and I'll arrest them."

Sapp wheezed. "Toole, you're a card."

Mimi felt like kicking him. The reek of him permeated the whole office, fouling the air.

Santiago worked the other sterilized gold plate into the hole above the ear, fitting scalp over it, muttering to himself.

"Perhaps this won't work and you'll croak," he said. "You can help me. What are your plans? Where are you going?"

Sapp rumbled, an earthquake in the rocker, and wheezed. "A card, doc."

Toole knotted Sapp's hair over the second plate. "I've used your hair to hold the plates and pull scalp over them. When it grows out, cut the knots away," he said. "I'll bandage this to cover it, and you can hope the scalp grows over the edge of the gold plates and anchors them in. Keep it bandaged for a couple of weeks. Keep it clean under there when you change the bandages—if you change them. I'll give you a little permanganate of potash and some cotton."

At Toole's nod Mimi released the rocker and it creaked up. Sapp peered at her with a gaze so palpably calculating that she felt dirtied by it, examined as meat. She glared back at him, this slaver of women, monstrous robber of soldiers, stealer of any property not nailed down.

"If the county fathers would ever finish building the jail I'd throw you in it, Sapp. And keep you there until I found grounds enough to hang you. But I don't. The county dithers away the days. I use the stone guardhouse at the Fort when I need to hold someone."

Sapp leaped up in wild alarm. "They'd kill me! Wiltz!"

He lapsed into sudden silence, while Santiago Toole stared at him, a faint smile at the corners of his mouth.

"That's a start. Five dollars, Sapp. Where'll you be? I should check on these in a few days."

"Gone, Toole," Sapp said. "For a few weeks, anyway."

That bit of news gladdened Mimi. She couldn't bear the thought of this monster in Milestown.

"I'm done, Sapp," said Toole. "I'll see if the coast is clear."

Santiago slipped out, and Mimi realized for the first time that the window shade had been pulled down tight.

She felt uneasy being in the same room with that man, but met his blank, dead-eyed stare with her own.

"All women are the same," he said. "All are useful."

Toole motioned Sapp to follow, and led him through darkened rooms and out the back door. She didn't wait. She yanked the curtains open and the sash up and flooded the room with sweet, clean night air. Outside, crickets hummed. A wolf howled, oddly close.

Toole returned and she buried herself in his strong arms. "Santiago, Santo, be careful. *Mon Dieu*, be careful."

She found herself sobbing, and hardly knew how it had started.

Chapter 7

At Fort Benton Mordecai Sapp hastened to the riverfront offices of the great mercantile company, I. G. Baker, where he kept his savings on account, and withdrew a thousand. Thence he repaired to the Overland Hotel, summoned a dressmaker, there being no tailor in Benton, and ordered clothing: two pairs of britches, a gray swallowtail with velvet collar, a brocade vest with special pockets in it, three shirts, smallclothes, and sundry other items not available in his size from the shelves of readymades. The dour woman sniffed about him suspiciously, eyed the massive bandage on his head, stared nervously at Popskull, and recorded his order in a flowery script. He volunteered extra pay if she'd employ other seamstresses to complete the first ensemble at once, in twenty-four hours, so he'd have new clothes.

Next, by telegraph, he ordered a faro layout, roulette layout, green baize poker and gaming tables, cards, and other sporting house equipment from Beman and Lansdale Furnishings in Denver City, letter of credit to follow.

Back at I. G. Baker, he limped through the warehouses—the company's Fort Benton facilities were largely used to transship goods from the river packets to the mining towns throughout the northwest—and purchased ready-made shoes, a greatcoat, a dozen sheets, bed ticks, crockery, two Stevens shotguns plus buckshot-loaded shells, one Smith and Wesson revolver, a boot knife, kerosene lamps, bar glasses, door and window hardware, three chamber pots, porcelain washbowls and pitchers, buckets, panes of glass, wooden chairs, a fancy chandelier, and numerous small items.

That accomplished, he took himself to a barber for a shave and bath, regretting that he must dress himself in his rank clothing until the new had been stitched together.

"What happened to your head?" the man asked.

"Industrial accident."

In a tub in a back room Sapp scrubbed off foul layers of filth and blood with his good right hand, threw away his small-clothes, and dressed again, feeling somewhat cleaner beneath his dirty black pants and old chesterfield.

"The water was too cold," he said, declining to tip the barber.

Then he and Popskull prowled the river town, eyeing the newly arrived paddlewheelers along the levee, some from as far as St. Louis but most of them up from Bismarck, where they'd brought goods shipped that far on the NP. *Key West. Eclipse. Nellie Peck. Helena.* Cordwood and buffalo hides lined the levee. The old adobe fur company post had become an army depot, manned by a contingent from Fort Shaw, and the rest of the bustling town a shipping center, with arteries reaching in all directions. Along Front Street the merchant establishments, I. G. Baker, Carroll and Steele, T. C. Power, Chouteau House, rubbed shoulders with saloons and grog shops, markets and saddleries. Back a way, nestling against the yellow bluffs, hulked the squat houses of the Row. He eyed them professionally but thought to visit them when he was attired properly.

At the Overland Hotel he ordered a double helping—one ate whatever was served—and shared the feast with Popskull, who wasn't a bit particular. He dozed in a real bed that night, lamenting the cost of all this but thinking in terms of Opportunity. The warm dark, and the breezes lifting the gauzy curtain at the open window, started him planning. Rebuild. But not just another dive. He'd go for the railroad trade when it came through, making more in a few months than he'd spend here furnishing a gaudy sporting palace. After that, the drovers. Those railhead towns in Kansas had wrung fortunes from the cattle drovers. They'd driven steers for months; booze-starved, woman-starved, good-times starved, when they were paid off they blew everything in one wild spree. Sapp looked forward to that in the summers, soldier customers year around, and in a few years he'd sell the dump and head for the lights. . . .

The woman brought the first of his duds and waited tight-lipped while he slid into them behind a Chinese screen. A white shirt. She had to help him because his left arm barely worked. Ivory brocaded vest over his vast torso. Black trousers. Stiff gray coat with velvet collar and certain small pockets where pockets shouldn't be. The pants seemed baggy and a little short, but he dismissed her. No more waiting. He paid some of the tariff and sent her off to complete her task. Ah, a man of parts, except for the ugly bandage over his skull, and the blackness under his eyes that persisted to speak of a close squeak with death.

Now for the real business, he thought, admiring his formidable image in a looking glass. Benton had everything for every appetite—even Sapp's. A veritable fountain of goods in a vast wilderness, he thought, limping heavily. He lacked a cane or walking stick, and made that his next business. T. C. Power had one, with a gold-plated head on it and a spring-loaded dagger in its base. Ah, worth it, worth it, he thought, shelling out seven dollars and fifty cents.

The day had been hot, but not so bad here beside the restless Missouri River as down in Milestown, where the July sun would be blistering the land and the town. He waited through the long summer twilight, lavender and apricot here in the intimate gulch carved by the river, until indigo night settled over Fort Benton. His business would be night business, and it might consume several days. From his previous prowling he'd narrowed down the choices to three saloons: Meyer's, The Redeye, and The Diamond Hitch. He thought to try them in that order. Meyer's was a log and canvas affair squatting uptown on the river side of Front Street, its rear poking out on piles over the swirling river itself—which Sapp admired. A good way to get rid of things—urine and dead bottles among them.

He limped west, his black enameled stick biting the hard earth, past silent, bumping packets with chimneys stabbing the stars, past closed butcher and harness shops, past scurrying men on furtive business, arriving at last at the batwings that served as a summer door. He turned in, leaving Popskull skulking outside. He found little light to guide him toward his pre-planned destination, a wall table, preferably in a corner, where he could nurse a foamless, varnished beer and observe.

No such seat existed here. A patron could stand at the bar or sit at a gaming table at the rear, the latter faintly ambered by suspended lamps. The light oozed from the lamps so dimly that he couldn't see what he needed to see, so he left. The Redeye, up a bit, proved better for his purposes. A bench of split cottonwood lined the wall opposite the bar, and a few splintered tables stood before the bench. Sapp slid into a corner, ordered, and studied the denizens there through a haze of blue smoke and just enough lamplight; they, in turn, studied him, as he wanted them to do. He looked like a mark; he looked rich; he looked not quite respectable. All this he knew about himself, and counted on.

Rough men. Hard men. Intimacy with the outdoors stamped their weathered faces. Muleskinners, bull-whackers, and woodcutters. Not exactly what he was looking for. He could tell by the eyes. The eyes gave every man away. He sipped sour beer, watched men play desultory five-card stud, watched them come and go, joke, josh each other, or sit silently. Some eyed him curiously from time to time, but no one came, no one talked. He expected that. A fat man in gambler's attire didn't really interest these outdoor men.

He waited out an hour and left. Far upriver he found The Diamond Hitch, a different and more familiar sort of sporting establishment; well lit by ten-lamp chandeliers of cut glass, serving women with opiated stares and a lot of leathery white bosom and varicosed leg showing, and games, games, games, operated by thin, bored men who never blinked. Even a mahogany bar, hauled off some packet, with real mirrors above the backbar, two cracked and one with the silver plate behind it decayed and smoky, the better for a bartender to observe the passage of all and the sudden movement of hands. Here a man dressed as he was, in an immaculate swallowtail and pearly brocade vest, with a fake glass headlight diamond he'd picked up, along with a gold-plated copper ring sporting a glass solitaire from a baubles tray at Power, seemed a part of the scenery. Others like him, only thinner, lounged everywhere, sizing him up and wondering about his purse and whether he'd settle at a faro bank or poker table or monte game, or pinch the girls, or offer to buy a drink.

Mordecai Sapp did none of these things. He lumbered painfully—walking had become an ordeal ever since lead had severed various connections in his skull—to a barstool clear around the far corner of the bar, next to where the hustling girls got their barrel whiskey from the two thin barkeeps pouring from Kentucky bottles. There he settled, his back to the wall, able to observe bartenders at work, the tired girls with hollow eyes and decayed white flesh, and the gamblers at their swift, sharp trade. Silent. A silent place, The Diamond Hitch, with a clientele as preoccupied with gain as the housemen and girls. Why not, he thought. Money makes a man serious.

He nursed Old Crow, poured from an uncorked green bottle, and knew it wasn't really Old Crow and that he wouldn't protest. In fact, he admired the management. Money and silence. He sat until his own bulky mass tired out his buttocks, studying everyone even as they casually studied him. He left around midnight, after two drinks and nothing more. He'd walked past the silent faro layout, where a night owl grimly resisted the final plucking, past the roulette and the poker tables run by observant men with eyes that licked him, past the dollies as if they didn't exist. No one edged close to him as he limped to the Overland, because the gunmetal blue in his right fist shone in the starlight, and a large gray wolf heeled beside him.

The next night, while he nursed a rye and branchwater at the Redeye, fortune smiled. A fat man, like himself, one he'd seen glancing at the backbar of The Diamond Hitch. A man deceptively soft, who fostered that misimpression for purposes of his own.

He entered, a soft, white-skinned, indoor man in a rumpled sable herringbone suit, utterly out of place among the weather-sculpted denizens of that saloon. He glanced around, spotted Sapp, and approached at once.

"May I?" he asked softly, nodding to the hard bench beside Sapp.

Sapp nodded, curious. Less literate men would have said "Can I?" The man settled at Sapp's left, staring out.

"I saw you at The Diamond Hitch."

"I saw you."

"You are not a player," the man said. "A minister, perhaps."

Sapp nodded. A barkeep approached.

"I don't drink spirits," the man said. "A sarsparilla."

"No," said the bartender.

"A drink, then."

A little later the bar man brought him pekoe-colored tea and charged the one-bit drink price. The man smiled softly. He lifted the glass, and set it down idly.

"I'm a broker," the man said. "I discover needs and fill them. You have needs."

Sapp studied the soft man, finding the deception, and enjoyed the thoughts that crowded into his mind. "I'm an entrepreneur," he said.

"I thought so."

"I have needs. What do you supply?"

The man laughed, a thin falsetto.

"My establishment burnt. I will rebuild, much better and fancier."

"An accident." It wasn't a question.

Sapp smiled and touched his bandage. The man read tea leaves.

"I'll need . . . a general manager."

The man smiled, cherubic and pink in the amber light.

"I'd also like you to deliver sergeants. Corporals, too. Can you deliver sergeants? Except for one. I'll deliver one."

"That would be new to me," the man said. "But I have faith."

"And a price."

The man lowered his gaze, diffidently.

A half hour later, Sapp had his man. A man who surprised him. He'd been looking for yellow wolf-eyes. He had envisioned a wolf-eyed man for his purposes. He knew all men by their eyes, and the lance of their gaze, but this one, Januarius Quigby, had fooled him. No wolf-eyes at all, no predator eyes, but the smudged brown eyes of a fat boy, gazing vapidly about, unseen. It startled Sapp that he could be so wrong. Quigby had all the qualifications, and was flexible as to the contract, wanting spending money plus large bonuses. He'd never dealt with the military before. And for sure, no noncom had ever dealt with a Quigby. It amused Sapp, a sergeant meeting pudgy Januarius Quigby.

Sapp had one remaining item of business, and he found that Quigby's intimate knowledge of the back alleys of the territory would enable him to conclude matters successfully.

Six dollies. Better than the ones he'd bought for the pig farm because he would open a higher-class joint, the better to suck the gold from better-paid marks. Hard to find on the Montana frontier. He'd feared he would have to go to Denver City, or maybe take the long stage ride to Bannack or Virginia City, both waning now. But Quigby had his own ways and means.

"Alder Gulch is dying and Bannack's down to hard-rock mining and company men with families. The ladies are suffering," he said.

"Buy some."

"Ah, no, Preacher Sapp. These are free agents. They come and go. They marry down. They retire upon their earnings."

Sapp grinned. "Buy them."

"They'll flee your chicken coop."

"Not with you roostering, Quigby. Not with our hand in their stuffed ticks."

"I'll get them and bring them across by coach, Reverend Sapp. There's the matter of expenses and fees."

Sapp winced. At I. G. Baker the next morning he withdrew more in the form of letters of credit, and saw Quigby off on the daily Helena stage. He picked up the rest of his new attire, still stiff with sizing, and deducted ten percent for slovenly sewing. The dour woman stared bleakly.

"You would," she said, "and no recourse for a poor woman."

"All women are useful."

He consigned his mound of goods to a Diamond R bullwhacker outfit heading for Miles, and caught a stagecoach back to Miles City, paying passage for Popskull on the roof.

He debarked with his wolf seven miles west of town. He didn't want to be seen in Milestown, but he also had other plans.

There, on small flats and river bottoms, Norwegian settlers were clearing away the cottonwoods to begin small ranches that would rely on the bottoms for hay and the bronze bluffs behind them for pasture. They had arrived in May and still lived in wagons and tents. Sapp paused in the rose light of a late July afternoon, admiring their progress. He remembered to doff his swallowtail and hide his fake headlight diamond, and then limped up the lane in his soaked-armpit shirtsleeves.

A dozen or so families, he guessed, with names like Svensrud, Fjare, and Rostad. Few spoke English, and that would be just fine. Not a one of them had ever put his foot in Hogtown, and that suited him also. He limped among them, trying three camps where men stared blankly and women squinted suspiciously. Then at last he found one where he might be understood, a place where a large log building was rising.

"Tollefson, Ole Tollefson," said a gaunt man with round spectacles in silver rims, who kept eyeing Popskull nervously.

"Ah, Quigby." He settled his heavy, sweating bulk on a log, to rest his lame leg. "I'm looking for carpenters. I pay well. A lot of carpenters at once, working fast, or I'll go elsewhere."

Tollefson listened politely, clucking and muttering. Sapp liked the looks of him, lithe and competent. They all understood wood. Put a Norwegian near wood and he'd do something splendid with it. Maybe their heads are made of it, he thought. He laid out his proposition: build him his saloon and hall across the river—he planned to erect it a hundred yards or so from the ruin of the old—this time of board and batten, classy-looking, real roof rather than log and sod, false front. Do it in a month for three dollars a day per man, half now. Plus a small separate cottage for himself. Hire every man and boy—seventeen of them, he learned—if they all worked hard.

"Ja, ja, maybe we could do that, Herr Quigby."

Sapp waited while Tollefson gathered the others and they debated in their northern tongue. He thought they'd do it. They lacked cash and he was offering them cash. It meant starting their own houses late in the year, but cold was nothing Nordics feared. And they could use the money to buy something to feed on in the winter, or livestock and seed in the spring.

"Three-fifty and sabbaths off, ja? You will supply the boards from the sawmill and nails and hardware, ja?"

Mordecai Sapp muttered and calculated, winced and grumbled, and agreed. He'd get it all back in a month when the tracklayers came through.

They shook on it in a russet dusk, and Sapp filled in some blanks in one of his letters of credit on I. G. Baker in Fort Benton.

"Uffdah, what have I done?" Tollefson said. "Now this waits, ja?" He waved at the rising log walls.

"What's that? A hall?"

"That is a *kirch*—church. The church of our country. We build it first, ja? The house of God. Then the rest."

Mordecai suddenly was glad he'd been cautious. A saloon and dance hall, he'd called his project.

"One last thing, Tollefson. Not a word. You are working for Quigby, get that? Januarius Quigby. But if anyone asks, you don't know." He grinned gently.

Tollefson stared, then nodded.

"A bonus if you finish by September 1, Tollefson. Five dollars a man." He wanted to catch the drovers when they arrived here from Texas.

Tollefson drove him to Miles in a battered wagon, through a chill night of the waning summer, and dropped him at the Nelson Miles Hotel, which passed for uptown in the brawling village. The sallow old clerk stared at his bandage, said nothing, and registered him as Januarius Quigby. He insisted on a room overlooking the street, and settled there with his new pigskin valise stuffed with baronial attire.

There'd be things to do in the morning: contract for wood and hardware and hauling. Rent a wagon at the livery barn and ride out to Hogtown after dusk, choose a site. Visit Toole and perhaps get rid of the turban that still swathed his head.

Not tomorrow, he thought. Tonight. The darkness would conceal the living dead from the army, from Sergeant Wiltz.

Chapter 8

Santiago Toole knew he'd become hard to live with and grouchy as a bitten dentist. He settled back into his routine sullenly while Mimi studied him with hard eyes, went Indian on him by muttering to herself in Assiniboin, switching to doe-skin dresses, and disappearing for long stretches, all unexplained. Sapp had vanished, and good riddance. If justice prevailed, he'd croak. But two things still rankled. Justice undone, and Wiltz's subterranean threat to annihilate him.

As for justice, he'd run out of clues and no one cared the slightest about what had happened at Hogtown. The massacre went unpunished and the guilty probably considered themselves heroes of sorts, or at least the types who solved problems. So Santiago settled into his daily routine, his odd wedding of medicine and law; walking his morning rounds and night rounds with a sharp eye for trouble; doctoring by day. A bad case of erysipelas in a woodcutter, which he treated with glycerin and a blood tonic consisting of fifteen-drop doses of a tincture of muriate of iron. A sudden onslaught of old Lyman French's chorea. A dangerous outbreak of diphtheria in the Woodmansee children, Max and Hilda, whose throats he swabbed with a mixture of chlorate of potash, syrup of orange, muriate of iron, and water. Lars Nelson's chronic ague, which Santiago treated with sulfate of quinine and extract of smartweed. San Antonio Rose's profuse yellowish discharges, leukorrhea, which he could do little for except prescribe rest, warm douches, and application of a compound of glycerin, sugar of lead, carbolic acid, laudanum, and water injected with a fountain syringe. And a flare-up of Titus Bass's consumption, for which he prescribed a fluid extract of veratrum viride for fast heartbeat and belladonna for night sweats. And Dover's Powder, three to five grains, if he needed it.

That plus a crate of stolen chickens, a fistfight among teamsters in the parlor of Texas Maude's, the discovery of the corpse of an unknown elderly male vagrant, with an empty blue bottle of paregoric lying near him in the river-brush, and the odd presence in Milestown of pairs of side-armed corporals, a blue-bloused loitering that never ceased. They made a point of lolling outside Toole's gingerbreaded white cottage, which served—until the county built him an office—as sheriff's office as well as doctor's. A threat, and one reason that Santiago's nerves were stretched taut. His evening rounds became more ominous. He tried doors, peered into gloomy shop interiors, swept around the backs of dark buildings, while the army, or a small part of it, lurked behind him, ahead of him, in shadows as he approached. Once he heard the dry click of a falling revolver hammer and jumped. The next night the snap of hammers rattled him four times. He slipped his own Remington from its holster, and when the next hammer dropped in an inky alley behind Frank Reese's Dance Hall, he fired high, a loud crack in the blue night, a flare. A warning to Wiltz to lay off.

That is how things went until he chanced to run into his friend and colleague Adelbert Hoffmeister, pulp-nosed post surgeon, who was buying a razor strop and mustache wax at Rank's. The army had been unable to recruit an adequate surgical staff, so Congress authorized it to employ seventy-five civilian doctors, among them Hoffmeister.

"I suppose you're cleaning out your infirmary now, Adelbert," Santiago said.

"Hardly."

"I thought perhaps with Hogtown burnt . . ."

"Ach! They maim themselves other ways more—bad diet. Scurvy still, a hundred forty years after Lind tried limes. I bark at Wade and he shrugs. Injuries. Piles. Colic. Scrofula. Bilious fever. Dysentery because they don't clean the sinks. Ah . . . drunks. Liver."

Santiago understood the hesitation. Hoffmeister liked his schnapps and it had cost him a civilian practice.

"Your venereal cases down?"

"Too soon to tell. Maybe they pick it up in the rest of the palaces."

"They can't afford the parlorhouses, mostly, Adelbert."

"Gunshot, too. I got gunshot. A corporal his revolver cleaning. Ach! Stupidity! He forgets to pull out the rounds and in the arm himself he shoots. Shatters the humerus and nicks the brachial artery and loses so much blood I am thinking he is gone. An hour—over an hour from the time he shoots himself—to me they think to bring him, covered with blood."

"Who?"

"Corporal Cletus Horn. Confederate veteran."

"Who brought him, Adelbert?"

"Wiltz. Liggett. Polanc."

"When was this?"

Hoffmeister considered. "Maybe fifteen days ago. About when Hogtown burnt. Ach, that was good news, Santiago! We maybe a healthy post will have."

One of them shot? The thought galvanized Santiago. He'd go back there, search again. Another piece. If only he could put enough together to have a case.

"Maybe I'll come visit, doctor. And stop by my office any time. I'm rarely backed up."

The sight of lounging, blue-bloused men subdued his impulse, but he thought that with some stealth he still might do what he must. Dawn, then. He knew they abandoned Miles some time each night and didn't show up until his morning rounds. July dawn, then. But even before that, he'd saddle the bay and be there as the gray first light dissolved into color.

His internal clock awakened him just at four, his intended hour, and he slipped silently from the sheets. Mimi reached across, and muttered in Assiniboin.

Within minutes he'd dressed and slipped his revolver belt on, saddled the bay, and slid into the night, with only a thin slit of light along the northeastern lip of the prairies to guide him. He passed the slumbering fort and rode quietly onward, arriving at the Hogtown gulch in opaque gray light so obscure he could barely make out the black ruin. He tied the bay deep in the cottonwoods on the slope and waited, not particularly tense—he'd been unobserved, and this abandoned hollow drew no one other than a few curiosity-seeking soldiers.

He wasn't sure what he was looking for. One of the inmates had shot back at Horn, presumably after being shot. It pointed toward the pox-faced punk, full of the bravura of all gun hawks. The reluctant dawn gave him time to think, to envision in his mind's eye what might have occurred. The eastern horizon pinked and cast an eerie glow over the ruin. He could see. He slid quietly toward the ruin of Sapp's cabin, feeling dawn breezes worry his hair, and began to dig quietly, poking with a stick. It didn't take long. Buried under the charred ash of a window sash, two feet from where the punk's pallet had been, he found a fire-dulled revolver, its walnut grips burnt off and its cartridges exploded. Dropped about where a hand flung over the edge of the bunk would have dropped it. He knew intuitively the Colts had shot the corporal. He picked it up gingerly, wishing he'd brought a rag to wipe it, and carried it two-fingered back to his bay, dropping it in his left saddlebag.

He intended to hunt more, now that he was here at a safe hour. So many questions. A lark trilled a morning song. The fate of the women absorbed him. He probed where their small dark cribs had been, poked through ash, finding bits of crockery, basins and pitchers, the remains of a looking glass. A curling iron. A tarnished double eagle. Brass buttons. In the saloon area he found a square Arbuckle coffee can, a knife with no handle, a corkscrew. A zinc sink used to rinse glasses. None of these had a story to tell.

He wandered around the area, studying rain-cleansed mud and bunchgrass, all the while nerving himself for the thing that had to be done. At last he cinched up the saddle on the bay and steered the animal east, toward Fort Keogh. The morning was young, and he wondered how long this July day would stretch.

The Fort seemed less sinister as he reined the bay toward it. The horse smelled animals, and its ears perked forward. Far off Toole spotted movement and dust clouds, and as he rode closer he made out a mule train just pulling out toward the south, with distant curses eddying back to him. Distribution day, he thought. Down a few miles on the Tongue, several bands of Sioux and Two Moons' Cheyenne camped; nominally friendly, actually prisoners of war. The Fort fed them, and that's what he found himself observing this morning. The smell of prairie dust, acrid in the breeze along with the odors of sweated men and beasts, drifted to him. He rode silently into the parade, past scowling barracks with dark windows gaping sullenly. Nothing stirred. The distant officers' row seemed as somnolent as the rest, save for two wives gossiping near playing children on the lawn in front of them.

He steered toward the infirmary, tied the bay to a post hitch there, slipped his saddlebags off, and entered.

Dr. Hoffmeister looked astonished. "You? But the hour is so early—I've hardly started my rounds."

"I'd like to talk to Corporal Horn. About the gunshot wound." Santiago liked that. It sounded medical, but he hadn't ridden out here to talk shop.

Hoffmeister's burly brows rose. "Why not?" he said. "I am on my rounds. You want to talk about gunshot. Observe his fingers and tell me what you think. Maybe tea later, yes?"

"Where is he?"

Hoffmeister pointed toward a small ward. Apparently noncoms rated some privacy.

Santiago found Horn slumped in a wicker wheelchair next to a bed being straightened by an orderly. His arm was encased in a plaster cast and in a sling, with only his dirty fingers poking out. The orderly finished, eyed the sheriff, and wandered off.

"I'm Doctor Toole, from town."

The corporal eyed him dourly, from eyes smudged black.

"I'm also the sheriff, as you can see."

Horn's eyes flicked briefly to the steel star pinned on Santiago's tight, smooth vest.

"Have something to show you, lad," he said, unbuckling a saddlebag. From within, he lifted the smoke-blacked revolver with the burnt-off grips. Horn eyed it, expressionless.

"This is what put that bullet into your arm."

Horn's eyes met his. "Ah don't know what you're talking about."

"Of course you do. This is the kid's weapon. He got one

shot off before you killed him. One cartridge here is dimpled from the firing pin. The rest exploded in the heat. I figure you fired at least three rounds. I have three spent bullets anyway."

Toole waited, studying the man, whose face had gone wary and tight.

"He almost killed you. You'd think getting winged is safe enough, but sometimes it isn't. Not when it punctures an artery and you almost bleed to death. Too bad they didn't get you back sooner. They let you sit around and bleed to death while they burned the place, shot the women, and dug a grave."

"Ah don't know where you heard that crap."

"There's a living witness, among other things."

"Bull," the man snarled. "Impossible."

Santiago smiled.

"Get out of here or Ah'll call the captain of the guard. No damned civilian is going to—"

"Shhh," said Santiago. "There's more. Can you move your fingers? Try it, lad. Let me see."

"Ah can't. They don't work."

"What does Dr. Hoffmeister say?"

"He says wait until the cast is off and Ah can exercise. But then—probably it won't work. He thinks the nerve—"

"Will the army hang on to a one-armed corporal?"

The man shrugged.

"I don't think so. Shortly you'll be honorably discharged. Then you'll be a civilian."

The corporal's expression darkened again.

"It's hard to get excited about someone murdering that punk killer, even if someone sneaked in at night and shot him as cold-bloodedly as if he was a rabbit. No. But murder is murder, Corporal. Planned, premeditated murder, too. They stretch nooses for that. What I want is the killers of those women. You tell me what happened, give me some names, and I'll do my best to keep you out of trouble when the law lands on those of the men who did this thing."

Horn laughed sarcastically. "Ah thought you had a witness."

"I need corroboration."

"You're saying that you'll nab me the moment Ah'm discharged and off the military reservation—unless Ah tell you things.''

Toole smiled.

''You don't even have a jail.''

''Who says I'll arrest you?''

''Do you think you'll find out when Ah'm discharged, and come get me, Sheriff? You think Ah don't got friends? Who'd bust you to bits? You think that tin star can buck the army?''

Toole smiled again.

''You're full of it, Toole. You bring your witness over and let the CO and Wiltz have a talk with him.''

''Wiltz let you bleed to death, almost.''

''That's a risk a soldier takes, Sheriff.''

''Who shot the women?''

''They'll bury me before Ah'd—don't know what you're talking about, Toole.''

''Very well, lad.'' Toole settled the burnt revolver in his saddlebag and stood. ''The penalty for murder is hanging—'hung by the neck until dead.' You tell the story to me now and I think you'll walk out. Think about it. I'll try again later. . . . Of course, if you can wiggle those fingers and use that arm again, you're safe—maybe. Go ahead, wiggle them.''

Santiago watched the lifeless hand, while Horn glowered.

Toole found Dr. Hoffmeister, declined tea, and left. He rode across the sunny parade unmolested and got back to Miles a short time later, in time to check on Mrs. Gatz, eight months along and expanding normally, and then scribble new information in his lengthening private account of the Hogtown affair.

That afternoon, the army arrived in Miles. Specifically, one squad of enlisted men and five noncoms, all under the personal direction of Sergeant Major Vernon Wiltz. One corporal and two enlisted men rode borrowed cavalry mounts, and these he posted at the east end of town to halt the escape of anyone bent on escaping. The rest of the men he organized into search parties of threes at the west edge, and gave them instructions.

He'd learned of Toole's interview with Horn only minutes after the sheriff had ridden off the post. Toole knew too damned much. The thought didn't alarm Wiltz. Nothing alarmed him.

The army, he'd learned long ago, was a flexible and powerful tool to be used in any way imaginable, within certain boundaries well understood by any senior sergeant worth his stripes. Power. That's what a body of armed men possessed.

"I've a little field exercise planned for the afternoon, Colonel," he'd said to Wade. "I hear a lot of government-issue stuff can be found in Miles, all of it stolen from us. Now, I've been thinking: let's get it. A few noncoms and a squad, house-to-house search. Might even turn up a deserter or two."

Wade had frowned. "No deserter'd be crazy enough to stop at Miles, Wiltz. No. I forbid it. They'd be in an uproar over there, soldiers pawing through their houses. They have rights."

Wiltz had counted on that response. He always asked for more than he wanted. "Oh, sah, private homes don't matter so much. I think we'll uncover a mound of stuff in the saloons, the parlorhouses, the merchant places—hotels, dives, dumps. sah, the places of public accommodation. Offices. Nothing private, sah."

Wade had frowned. "That'd be trouble enough. They have rights too, I'd remind you. How much do you think you'd recover?"

"Upwards of five thousand dollars' worth, sah. Not counting rustled cavalry mounts with bad brands."

Wade had drummed pale fingers on his desk, and finally smiled faintly. "I'm going to give you written orders this time, just in case. They will authorize you to examine public places and confiscate stolen army materiel. They'll expressly prohibit entering private residences or harassing any citizen. That's going far, Wiltz. If you stir up trouble, it's your ass."

Minutes later, Sergeant Major Wiltz was tucking his copy of the orders in his blouse pocket and beginning to organize his foray. Stolen materiel was not his goal, although he hoped to collect enough to justify the raid. If not, he had ways and means of producing enough to satisfy the CO. No, this would be something else: a hunt for Toole's alleged witness—who probably didn't exist—and a little visit with Toole, who seemed unusually slow-witted and needed another lesson. If Toole protested, it'd be all the easier.

"We'll start with the parlorhouses," he announced to his men. "Everything government-issue we keep, no matter how they say they got it. There'll be a corporal or sergeant with every searching party looking for deserters. I'm wandering down to the sheriff's office, and you'll find me there."

Deserters weren't exactly what the noncoms would look for, he knew. Toole had told Horn about a witness. Twice now the sheriff had mentioned a witness. Probably nonsense, Toole's own little game. But it would pay to turn the town inside out, just in case someone—anyone—connected with Hogtown had survived.

He watched the search parties spread out, one to Texas Maude's, another to The Golden Calf, another to The 44, run by Mag Burns. Maude's was highest class and had pretty girls. A few officers patronized the place, and it pleased Sergeant Wiltz that he might have a few new levers to pull when all of this was done. The sounds of outraged womanhood drifted to him from open windows, and he laughed. They were expert cussers, those dollies, and the music on the July breezes came sweet to his ears.

Texas Maude herself stomped out into the sun, wearing a turquoise silk kimono, spotted the sergeant major, and stormed toward him dagger-eyed.

"What's the meaning of this?"

She'd been in the business for years, but somehow looked golden and succulent even with crow's-feet around her eyes and varicose-veined ankles. Wiltz eyed her thick, shapely form under the thin silk.

He yawned. "Routine search."

"Routine! You're stealing my stuff. You're robbing my girls."

"The Fort's missing a lot of things."

"That's not what I'm talking about! They're taking my girls' gold and greenbacks."

"Sorry, Maude, but I believe you're running a public nuisance."

"You sonovabitch!" she spat. "I'll get even."

Wiltz grinned. She whirled back to her house.

One of the search parties had started on the saloon row, and he watched it disappear into Bug's. He didn't expect much from saloons. The real squawking would start when they hit the merchants, and started digging through storage rooms. Like Gatz, who peered out the front door of his emporium, wondering about the ruckus. The merchant saw Wiltz and plowed toward him, his bald head glowing in the sun.

"What is this, Sergeant?" he demanded, waving his hand at the mounting chaos.

"Little search," Wiltz said, grinning.

"Who gave you authority? You have search warrants?"

Wiltz smiled. Pretty soon he'd be seeing Toole.

Chapter 9

Mimi rode home after a satisfying morning. She'd been feeling her Assiniboin blood recently, for reasons she couldn't fathom. Toole had gotten on her nerves. Not just Toole. His whole world. White men's civilization. Houses, parlors, mercantiles, schools, churches, and people who lived as if a millstone crushed them, keeping them from being themselves. White men hardly even got happy or mad, she thought scornfully.

Santiago had proposed, and in the proposing torn her into her two bloods, though he didn't know that. The advancing hot summer had started her singing, like a caged bird, the song of her mother's wandering life, the laughter beside cottonwooded creeks, the buffalo hunts, the freedom—at least the freedom they'd once had before the whites had invaded the land and killed the buffalo.

She'd caromed off of Santiago's rooms like a caged thing. She'd wandered the streets of Miles, shunned by most people who either knew her for a breed or thought her entirely Indian. Sometimes now she resented Santiago, and even resented his abiding love, for it imprisoned her all the more. She'd wanted to walk north, north across wide prairies, to her mother's people. Desolation now. That was their lot, the lot of all tribes who happened to be in the way of the restless whites.

She'd started riding, riding through the white days of high summer, riding astride Indian-style, her voluminous gingham skirts hiked high up her golden legs. She'd plaited her jet hair and let the braid run down her back. She'd started to wear a bear-claw necklace, and on cooler days a doe-skin blouse dotted with elk teeth, her mother's prized possession.

Then she'd remembered the camps of the Sioux and Cheyenne up the Tongue, and had ridden there to be among her own. Not really her own, these hereditary enemies. Not really her own: Her French blood and her convent education in the East placed a silent wall between herself and those people. But she'd ridden there frequently, made friends, and had been welcomed. She'd listened to bitterness and frustration, picked up their words readily, and soon found herself a citizen of these villages rather than Milestown. Her relationship to Santiago Toole puzzled and disturbed her all the more, as the summer breezes seduced her away.

Today was distribution day, and she'd ridden down to help and teach. They'd been throwing away flour in order to have the sacks, and then starving. She'd wandered among them, teaching Sioux women what to do with flour, how to make breads and cakes, even how to add gravy to meat. And more. She'd taught them about yeast and baking powder, lard and condiments. She'd translated and carried complaints to the soldiers, making sure the distributions had been evenhanded and fair.

She saddled and rode home early afternoon, satisfied, ready to nourish her other side, her white side, spend a while with her doctor, enjoy the caring that she found always in his blue eyes. That had been her lot in life, division, two worlds, ruthlessly pulling her apart. She rode up the west bank of the Tongue, past the distant fort lying to the west, and across the crude army bridge over the river on the trace to Milestown, and thence eastward toward the village that largely lived off Fort Keogh.

Even as she passed its farthest western precincts she sensed something amiss, odd, excited about Milestown. Angry men out on Main Street, arms jerking and flailing, their voices echoing against the wind. And over at the Row, girls outside. She'd rarely ever seen such women outside in broad daylight. Soldiers, too. In threes, she saw, methodically entering each shop and hauling things into a pile in the middle of the broad street. She tugged the reins to watch. Looting. The army seemed to be looting Milestown. Where was Santo?

The loudest hubbub erupted from the Nelson Miles Hotel,

and pierced even against the wind to her ears, sounds that defied the breeze. She touched her moccasins to the pony and it trotted forward, ears pricked forward and wary. The whole of Milestown's businesses lay in a single short block, which she entered, walking her paint pony slowly. Army things in the street. A pile of blankets. Hjorts Gatz of the hardware raging at a corporal, who looked amused and pushed the merchant back with the barrel of a Springfield carbine.

"I have bills of sale. Those are new Colts, fresh from the East! Check the serial numbers!"

"Looks like army to me," the corporal said, leering.

Mimi understood, suddenly. Most of these things would never be given to the quartermaster at Keogh.

From the hotel she heard fearsome cursing, banging doors, a woman's shriek, breaking glass, and the mock of soldiers. The blue-shirts! Some primordial fear gripped her, the fear of all the bronzed peoples of the plains when the bluecoats came to kill and loot. Only this time they'd visited a white man's village. Did they loot their own? she wondered. She hawked and spat at the yellow dust.

There, near the end of the block, stood the sergeant major, the one in charge, the one Santo had told her about. He stood like a rock, thick, rooted to the earth, a giant with a bullet head and a neck broader than his head, rooted like he owned the earth and everything on it, and all knees knelt before him. Like God.

She watched a corporal go to him. "No one in the hotel we're looking for," he said.

The sergeant responded with the faintest nod. He turned, glanced at her, and she felt the thick stare of his eyes rake her, settle on her hiked shirt and golden legs and moccasins.

"Get that squaw outa here," he said.

She heard, and touched moccasins to her pony, setting it toward home, which took her past the sergeant.

"You. Squaw."

She kept on riding. With a swift dart, surprising in a man so heavy, he flicked an arm out and caught the bridle.

"Where you going? How come you ain't back down the river? You savvy?"

"I'm on my way home," she replied quietly.

Her good English seemed almost to smack him in his chops. He didn't let go.

"You a Hogtown dolly?"

"I live here."

He grinned. "You didn't answer me, sweetheart. You don't live here, now do you?"

Fear crept through her. Never had she felt so helpless as in the clutch of this man.

"I'm on my way to my husband."

"Your husband! You probably have about fifty husbands. You got some shack or dugout around here, to take them all on?"

"I'm Mrs. Toole," she said, white-lying and wishing she'd listened to Santiago.

"Mrs. Toole, now." He squinted at her, and caught the eye of Gatz, who still argued furiously with a corporal and two privates.

"Gatz. Who's this squaw?"

The merchant stopped long enough to glance at her. "She's Toole's missus. Half-French. You fool with her and he'll kill you, Wiltz."

Sergeant Wiltz's face turned beatific, and his flat eyes slid over her, undressing her stitch by stitch. "Sheriff Toole's woman. A lusty bugger, that mick. Toole's woman."

She felt the cat's-paw weight of his gaze, and loathed it.

Sylvane Tobias erupted from his shop, with three blue-bloused soldiers behind him.

"What is this outrage, Sergeant?"

"Just a little checking up here, calling in a few debts."

"Why did these men invade my shop? Open each casket?"

"Deserters," Wiltz said.

"You're not looking for deserters!" Tobias raged. "You're looking for bodies with holes in them!"

Mimi watched the sergeant's feral eyes go gentle, and she chose that moment to break free. She kicked the pony savagely, a fine thump, and he careened forward. But Wiltz didn't let go of the bridle, didn't even tilt. He stood rooted like an oak, like a concrete hitching post with an iron ring in it, and her pony pivoted around.

"Sorry, ma'am," he said gently, and turned back to Tobias. "What do you mean by that?"

"I mean the whole town's figured what happened up the river and what you're covering up."

"And what would that be?"

"Murder," snapped Tobias. "Scum they were. Crooks they were. But when soldiers get to murdering poor slave women . . ."

Sergeant Wiltz grinned amiably, even as his massive fist cut upward into the cabinetmaker's gut, just under the ribs. The man gasped, folded to earth, his mouth a flapping hole that sucked no air. He spasmed, arced upward, his legs slowly stretching taut, his fingers clawing and stretching, his face graying. Then with a sigh, his body relaxed into utter quietness.

She screamed, a long, low howl.

Civilians and soldiers stared at Wiltz and the still figure of the cabinetmaker. She saw Toole, running. The sheriff glanced sharply at Wiltz, at her, at the quiet form settling deeper into the dung of the street. He studied Tobias swiftly and flipped the man over onto his stomach, straddled him and began rhythmic compressions of the man's lungs, pushing air out, letting them suck it back in, one minute, two. Life slid into Tobias as his paralyzed system began to function again. Men gathered, citizens and soldiers, but Santiago Toole paid them no heed. Sylvane Tobias's lungs pumped irregularly, spastically. His hands clutched and released, and color returned.

At last the sheriff stood. Nearby, Wiltz watched, his hand still clamped on the bridle of Mimi's pony.

"Wiltz," he said, some strain brittling his voice, "you're under arrest for attempted murder. Maybe it'll be murder if he dies."

The sergeant major seemed inscrutable, and Mimi couldn't fathom what was passing through his mind. Thirty or forty people had collected here now, drawn to violence like flies to offal, all of them male, some of them soldiers.

Sergeant Major Wiltz looked amused. "Take me in, Sheriff."

On the rutted dirt Sylvane Tobias rolled over and stared up at them, groaning gently.

Neither Toole nor Wiltz carried a sidearm.

"If you resist, I'll add that to the charges."

She saw Wiltz slowly surveying the mob. Not one civilian wore a weapon. Each blue-bloused soldier carried a sidearm, and the noncoms were slipping into a natural perimeter. Wiltz's huge left hand still grasped her bridle.

"Let go of my horse!" Mimi snapped.

He glanced toward her, and that's when it happened. Santiago's boot caught Wiltz squarely in the groin, with a thump that echoed a block. A whoof of air exploded from the sergeant major. His face went gray and he folded like a straightedge razor pivoting into its sheath, and reflexively clutched at his private parts, even while Santiago's fist smashed into Wiltz's chin, tumbling the sergeant major into the dust near Tobias. It shocked her. Men gaped. Santiago plucked a revolver from an enlisted man and buffaloed Wiltz as he slid to earth, a resounding crack on his skull that lacerated it.

Utter disbelief etched the faces of merchants and soldiers alike. David had slain Goliath. Santiago glanced bitterly at the writhing, half-conscious sergeant and then stepped back, swinging his borrowed weapon at the gaping soldiers.

"You!" he snapped at the corporal, his words stinging the air. "You! Hands up! All of you soldiers! Hands high! You over there, get in here with the others!"

The distant one, a corporal, smirked and stood still, his hand easing toward his holster.

Santiago's shot startled the whole crowd, and most hit the earth in fear of their lives. The bullet smacked into the corporal's holster with deadly accuracy, tearing leather and ripping through the grip of the revolver. The man yanked his hand away violently.

Mimi saw one noncom, a buck sergeant she'd never seen, ease swiftly behind Santiago's field of vision. "Santo, watch out behind!" she cried.

He whirled, his weapon stabbing relentlessly, his finger only a fraction from pulling the trigger. The skinny sergeant paled and slowly raised his hands.

"Lie down."

Reluctantly the buck sergeant did. Santiago swung the revolver around at the remaining shocked soldiers, still gaping at the fallen sergeant major as if they'd seen the Second Coming.

"Down," he snapped. "Hands out in front of you."

Wiltz stirred, and Santiago buffaloed him again. The sergeant major sighed and slid flat.

From the earth a corporal peered up at him. "You're dead, Toole. No tin-star sheriff mucks with the army. You're dead and buried but you just don't know it yet."

"We will take note of the murder threat," Santiago said tartly. The merchants still gaped, riven now with a fear that yellowed their eyes. The lot of them, most still hugging earth, seemed to want nothing more than to flee.

"Mr. Gatz, get up and get anything from that heap of stuff there that doesn't belong to the army. Write the serial number of each revolver you reclaim and I'll send the numbers back to Colonel Wade. . . . The rest of you. Pick up what's yours and leave what's the army's. If it's army-issue, I don't care how you got it, leave it. That's your loss."

Mimi's nerves settled a little, and surprise left her. Now that she thought about it, she remembered some things that Santo had told her one sweated night. His father the baron had started him mastering soldier skills as a boy, everything a man needed to know, clean and dirty. We're from a long line of killers, he'd told his son. That's how we became barons. Santiago had used those hard skills from time to time, and the people of Custer County had made him sheriff.

"Mimi," he said quietly, "fetch me my manacles, both pairs, and my Remington."

Reluctantly she wheeled her pony. She wanted to stay. She wanted to be extra eyes and ears for him. He still faced a dozen dangerous soldiers lying on the ground, all armed. She raced hastily to the house, leapt from her pony, and dashed in. The holstered revolver hung from a chair back. The manacles sprawled on a counter near his microscope. She snatched them and the revolver belt and hurried back to her pony, startling a black and white magpie into flight.

On her return nothing had changed much. Wet, dark sweat ringed the armpits of Santiago's shirt. Tobias was sitting up, looking desperately ill and gray. Sergeant Major Wiltz now lay on his back, golden dust and mustard manure clinging to his blouse, looking as dangerous half-awake as he did alert. The soldiers had grown restless and alert, glancing at each other, eye-messages. The town merchants had shrunk back, frightened. A few had vanished. The rest watched from the distant safety of porch shade in front of their stores.

"Think about it," Santiago was saying to the soldiers. "A lot of witnesses. Unless you murder every man who saw all this. There'll be an official inquiry. Courts-martial. Demotions. Maybe some guardhouse time. Maybe they'll turn you over for a civil trial, since you were stealing from civilians."

His voice throbbed sharp and Irish.

"You!" he snapped at a corporal. "What's your name?"

The corporal glowered, silent.

Mimi dismounted and handed his revolver belt to him. He shook his head.

"Put it on me."

She did, from behind, her arms snaking around him to buckle it at his waist.

"The manacles, Mimi."

He took one set of them with his free hand, backed around Wiltz's sprawled form where he could keep an eye on the prone soldiers, and edged up to the inert sergeant major.

He was reaching for Wiltz's wrists when the sergeant's legs kneed upward, catching Toole's torso. Wiltz's huge legs unfolded, shoved, tossing Sheriff Toole upward; higher, his arms flailing at air, and then hard to earth on his shoulder.

They landed on Santiago before he could get his wind. All of them, up off the ground, a blue wave, with Wiltz landing first, his massive purple fists battering Santiago Toole's face to pulp with swift brutal blows.

She screamed, and Wiltz glanced up at her, his feral eyes shining with some atavistic joy as he smashed blow after blow into the prostrate sheriff. Toole writhed and twisted and bled, bright crimson leaking from nose and mouth and ears. And still the blows never ceased. The others, too. Boots now, heavy army-issue boots smashing into the sheriff's bones. She heard his ribs crack. Something else snapped. They were killing him.

Two revolvers were lying about. She dived for one, caught its cold blue steel in her shaking hands and fired into the air. They barely paused. Trembling, she aimed it square at Wiltz and fired. He jerked as if stung by a nettle, grinned, and clambered off Toole, leaking blood from his armpit, leering. She shot at him again, missing because her hand shook so terribly. And then his giant paw smacked her, cracked her so hard she sailed through space, the revolver spinning away.

She felt his paws clamp her arms, some giant force pinning her. Behind him, she saw Toole slide into stupor and lie still, his shirt bloodsoaked, his face purple pulp, his legs akimbo, his chest spasming unnaturally with the vibrations of death.

He dragged her toward her home. The pony skittered away and followed along. She stumbled but it didn't matter: The massive force of his grip dragged her along as if she weighed less than a sheet of paper. The world whirled red and lemon and copper. Houses turned on their sides. The blue skies arced beneath her. Her heart bolted off. Every tug loosened her bones in their sockets. She heard laughter, and saw corporals and the other sergeant beside her, felt their hands lift her, felt her skirts fly up and more laughter.

They dragged her up her porch, skinning her shins on the steps, into her own house, Santiago's office, a-jumble with medical apparatus and dodgers and sheriff's things. They crowded in, peered around in the shadowed cool interior. She felt salty blood in her mouth, saw it drip over her skirts, smelled it and sweat and manure on Wiltz and the others, rank and acrid in the quiet gloom. He dropped her suddenly, and she tumbled to the floor, crumpling into an old Brussels carpet of Santiago's.

Wiltz strolled around, lifting and poking.

"Ah!" he muttered, and slid a handful of spent bullets off of Santiago's rolltop desk, pocketing them. He discovered the remains of a revolver with its grips burnt off, and handed it to a corporal. He poked around, seeing nothing else, glancing casually at Santiago's ledger, which she kept in her own hand—patient, treatment, and fee paid or owing. Time stopped while Wiltz stared.

"What's this? Head injury. Five dollars. June twenty. Here's another this month. No name. Head injury."

She glared at him silently. Wiltz laughed.

One of them dragged her to her feet and wordlessly shoved her back through the house, through their private parlor, back, finding their bedroom, and into that darkened place with its lavender scent and the faint fragrances of a spice sachet in her closet, mingled with sweat and blood.

"No," she wept, hot tears rising. No, no, no. Knowing it would be yes.

Chapter 10

Januarius Quigby, fresh off the bone-jarring stage from Bozeman City and points west, discovered himself already registered at the Nelson Miles Hotel.

"Ah!" he exclaimed mildly to the quizzical clerk. "My older brother has arrived before me. A man built like myself, yes?"

The clerk appraised Januarius, nodded, and handed Januarius the key. He plodded up the stairs and let himself in, discovering the bore of a derringer pointed at him as he entered.

"Ah, Reverend Sapp!" he said. The man had removed the grimy bandages about his porcine head, and over an ear something gold glinted peculiarly. He'd lost a lot of weight.

The bore lowered.

"I told the clerk we're brothers."

Sapp nodded. "What happened?"

"It turned out better than I'd hoped, Mordecai. I've recruited eight young ladies, each of them carefully examined for youth and beauty and, ah, tractability, and each eager to come. I hope we'll get six out of it. Two from Last Chance Gulch, and the rest from Virginia City. Things are going downhill in both places, and the ladies are all too eager to find better lodes to mine. Of course, I promised them everything—luxury, wealth, vast earnings, keep seventy-five percent, room and board free, in spacious new quarters. You, ah, will need to make some swift adjustments in their expectations once they arrive."

Sapp smiled benignly.

"I bought them coach tickets and told them to be here as

93

soon after the first as possible. These coaches are impossible, Reverend Sapp. They bruised my flesh and rattled my bones, and the food at the stations was—abominable. Ah, when the railroad comes, the luxury . . .''

Sapp looked pleased. He even managed to smile while Quigby went over the accounting, explaining how he'd spent more than intended and wanted more.

"Now then, Quigby," Sapp said coldly. "Things have been happening here, not all of them comforting. I've hired a gang of Norwegians to build the establishment and they are droning away at it. I've given them to the first, and here it's the fifteenth. In two weeks we open. That means, Quigby . . .''

"Call me Januarius."

Sapp glared, then relaxed. "Very well. But remember who's employing and who's employed."

Quigby shrugged, a dimple forming on his soft cheeks. It never mattered. He had utterly no sense of hierarchy, and did whatever he pleased always.

". . . that means I must take delivery soon."

The noncoms. Sapp wanted the noncoms dealt with before the opening. Exterminate the sergeants who would gladly burn the place again and kill everyone in it.

"Not much time," said Januarius. "I am a man who takes his time."

"We're not safe in this hotel, Quigby. Two weeks ago they swept the town. Wiltz, the sergeant major, plus some other noncoms and a squad of soldiers. Rousted every mortal out of every hotel and parlorhouse and saloon. Looking for deserters, they said. A joke. Looking for stolen army stuff. A joke also. Looking for me; for any survivors of Hogtown, actually, because of what that fool sheriff, Toole, had said.''

"Tell me about the sheriff."

"Toole? An Irish grandee. They're holding him at the Fort, in the infirmary. They beat the fool when he resisted. They've accused him of obstructing an army operation or something. There'll be an inquiry. When Wiltz is done, Toole will never see daylight again." Santiago smiled benignly.

"And you think the sergeants might sweep Milestown again. While we're here."

Sapp shrugged. "I've become a creature of the night. I don't show myself by daylight. A few merchants might recognize me. But there are some saloons. . . ."

Quigby considered. Two weeks. "Your carpenters are on time?"

"Ahead."

"You have your supplies. Redeye, beer, games, tables, all the rest?"

"Most of it. In the Diamond R warehouse."

Quigby smiled. "Then I'll be busy. You may not see me for a few days at a time. Give me names."

Sapp's eyes went soft. "Corporals Horn, Liggett, Polanc. Maybe LeMat. Buck Sergeant Buford. And Wiltz. Maybe others. LeMat and Polanc have wives and live in log cabins on suds row—their wives scrub." He smiled wanly. "All women are useful. Either for drudge or sport."

"We will talk about bonuses now," Quigby said meekly. He always addressed people meekly, a picture of gelded, pudgy reticence. And came away with twice as much from disarmed men.

A while later a portly, brown-eyed drummer, with smudge-soft eyes behind round rimless spectacles, emerged from the Nelson Miles Hotel carrying a fine new carpetbag with ashes-of-roses knap and harness-leather trim. He hired a hack from the day liveryman, Cornelius Porter, so as not to muddy his shining black patent-leather shoes, and set off for Fort Keogh, two miles and one river west of town.

He always enjoyed this part of it. Fate had bestowed upon him the perfect appearance for his calling: No gunman was Januarius Quigby, and in fact he disdained the gunmen he'd read about in Buntline's junk novels. How absurd to risk one's life to prove something or other. Even worse to let the victim or any bystander see you. Why exterminate a man when he faced you with a loaded weapon when you could do it much easier aiming at a point between the shoulder blades of his back? Why do the dance of death, the same dance over and over, when it paid to be unpredictable and never perform these little tasks twice in the same manner? And why appear in the public eye as some brawny, lean hawk of a man, a memorable man, when one's whole purpose was to be instantly forgotten, or even better, never even noticed?

All of these things Januarius Quigby had thought through carefully, and had perfected his trade in ways unheard of. Take for instance his genius for creating accidents. Why arouse the suspicion of lawmen if one could arrange a murder to look just like a catastrophe, a wreck, the hand of God? He smiled at that. The hand of God. He was getting rich fast, heaping money in an Albuquerque bank, but that had ceased to be his purpose in life. The stalk had become everything. A perfect record. Eighteen times now had he achieved his purpose, leaving no aftermath, no wanted posters, no descriptions, no suspicions. Eleven of these events had been perceived as accident, illness, or—he smiled again—cause unknown. He loved the latter. Cause of death unknown.

And why, for that matter, use firearms at all, when such a fine array of means lay at hand? Arsenic. Strychnine. Ice picks, knives, garrotes, and lead pipes. Not to mention overdoses of laudanum, missing bridge timbers, pulled-up rail spikes, blasting powder, unignited coal gas, plugged chimneys, a wood-stove log loaded with giant powder, food poisoning, crazed harness horses, and arson. He especially enjoyed arson, because it consumed any stray evidence and gave the victim time to think on his sins. Once he'd even achieved asphyxiation, by stuffing a banker into his vault.

He always used his real name. Pseudonyms, he supposed, led to difficulties and insincerity. As an independent drummer he had always maintained contacts with various suppliers of whatever goods he chose to peddle, and took pains to order goods and settle accounts periodically, for all the world to see. He could be anywhere he chose to be, selling whatever suited him, and impeccable always.

In Denver City he kept his beautiful dumpling daughter, now twenty years old, in a lavish ground-floor flat where she could maneuver her wheelchair out upon the gardens. Dawn. Dimple-cheeked Dawn. Her accident had changed his life as well as her own. Eight years ago when she'd been twelve, she'd been cavorting on the street one sunny Fourth of July when two big boys in brown corduroy knickers, sons of the police chief, set off a dozen giant firecrackers, cannon shots, that terrorized the drays of a horse-drawn trolley. They thundered out of control, struck his Dawn, felled her in front of the flanged steel wheels of the trolley, which severed her left leg below the knee. An alert doctor on the scene stanched the blood and saved her.

Januarius had sought redress from the chief, the city, and the trolley company, to no avail. And after a year of frustration he took matters into his own hands. The rowdy boys died suddenly of brain fevers; the chief a few months later of an ulcerating stomach; and the magnate who owned the trolley line of self-inflicted gunshot, or so they said. No one had ever suspected design in any of it. So, he thought, there could be justice in the world after all. He cared about that, and preferred cases in which he could feel the rank injustice of matters, and find some profound delight in destroying the unjust. It had become a sacred mission in his life, mending justice.

Quigby drove his dray past a smartly dressed guard, past buildings whose purposes he couldn't fathom, and out upon the dun parade, flanked on one side by officers' quarters being rebuilt in tan brick with mansard roofs, and enlisted men's barracks on the other. He would, he thought, take the measure of Wiltz first, and steered toward the obvious headquarters building, with the Stars and Stripes flapping in a hot wind, and regimental colors shimmering beneath it. As he hitched the dray with a carriage weight, he mulled the products in his carpetbag, wondering what he should be selling. Patent venereal remedies, he thought.

Why was Adelbert staring at him? He closed his eyes, opened them, and tried again. Adelbert, studying him like a butterfly collector pinning a new monarch.

"Adelbert?"

"Thank Gott."

"Where am I?"

"The fort infirmary, Santiago."

"Why?"

"You are hurt."

"I am?" Santiago tried to sit up but gasped as pain in a

dozen places lanced him, and settled back. He suddenly realized he was burning with fever, and nausea gripped him. "I am."

"You will make it now. For two weeks I sit and wait."

"Two weeks?"

"Longer, Santiago."

It amazed him. "What's wrong with me?"

Doctor Hoffmeister sighed, looking reluctant. "Just a few things."

"Dammit, I'm a doctor. Tell me."

Santiago could see the man hovering beside his bed turn that request over in his mind, sighing with the weight of decision.

"Very well, then. Three lower ribs broken, two left, one right. Your right lung punctured by the splintered rib on the right. Three teeth, two molars and one incisor. A cracked jaw, right side. Concussion. Possible skull fracture, parietal. Ear lobe missing, left ear. Facial lacerations. Left arm broken, ulna, but not a bad break. Contusions on that arm. High fever. Mashed fingers, one broken. Contusions of the kidneys— you've been passing blood. Other internal injuries I cannot determine. Internal hemorrhages. Liver damage. Contusions and lacerations on both legs; torn cartilage, broken toes, lacerations . . ." His voice trailed off into gutturals.

Santiago absorbed this glumly. He hurt, now that he thought about it. "How'd I get here?"

"Hjorts Gatz. He put you in a wagon. Everyone else thought you were dead. Kaput."

"Where's Mimi?"

Hoffmeister shook his head. "No one knows. She disappeared the day it happened. No one knows. . . ."

"Didn't she come here at all?"

"Never. I'm sorry."

"Then she's in trouble." He felt suddenly desperate, knowing he could not even sit up.

"Has anyone looked for her?"

"That I don't know. They've got no law over there and the thieves run wild. Maybe they will a deputy appoint. Meanwhile the army patrols."

"When can I . . ."

Hoffmeister shook his head. "You are lucky to live. And when you get up you can't go. You are under guard."

"I'm what?"

"There are accusations, Santiago."

Toole couldn't fathom this news and stared helplessly at his colleague.

"They—the ones who went there—say you obstructed an army dragnet and tried to prevent them from recovering stolen government things. . . . A grafter, they say." Hoffmeister shook his head. "I can't tell you more of this rubbish they swear. Or tell them you make a living as a doctor and don't need the graft. I can't—" Hoffmeister's gentle brown eyes filled suddenly. "I keep you alive, for what? For dishonor. Your heart stops and I start it and work your lungs, and for what? They don't believe me. Why should they believe an old drunk?"

Hoffmeister turned his head away.

Toole felt close to tears himself, and peered upward at his friend, helpless and afraid. Then, slowly, a realization seeped through him.

"Can Wiltz come here?"

"The sergeant major comes often and stares. I try to be here."

Santiago wondered, suddenly, whether he'd ever leave this place alive. Only Hoffmeister's presence kept the man from a quick fatal thrust.

"Who put the guard at the door?"

"The colonel. He's looking forward to an inquiry, a hearing about what happened. Already townsmen come to tell him things. What they say I don't know."

"I have to get out of here."

Hoffmeister shook his head.

"Who else comes here?"

"My orderlies. Gatz, he tried once to come but the CO wouldn't let him."

"Any other noncom?"

"Ach, the guard—the guards are corporals."

"Adelbert—my life's in danger. You've got to get me out. Now."

"A pierced lung. Blood in your urine. Blood in your stool. Concussion. Have you double vision?"

"No. . . ." Santiago calculated his injuries, totting them up like an accountant. Ten days or two weeks . . . He glanced toward the door, which stood ajar, seeing no one beyond.

"Adelbert," he whispered, "do you believe me, that my life's in danger?"

The post surgeon nodded.

"I need a revolver and a means to hide it, conceal it from the orderlies and others."

Hoffmeister shook his head furiously. "No! It is beyond—"

"Why bother to save me then?"

The surgeon looked trapped, and worried the thought like an old bone. "Maybe I can have you carried to my house. You need constant attention, which Mrs. Hoffmeister—" He thought better of the idea and shook his head. "No. But I will have the orderlies come here whenever anyone else comes."

Santiago felt despair and exhaustion creep through him, and closed his eyes. He heard Hoffmeister walk away, muttering things in small explosive shots of breath.

I could yell, Santiago thought, *if my lung would let me.* It hurt even to draw breath, a fire across his ribs. He had only the weapon of noise, and hardly that with a swollen cracked jaw, teeth missing, and wounded bellows.

He drifted back into the white world again, tumbling softly through ether. No laudanum. He'd been too close to the brink for that, and Hoffmeister had wisely steered clear. But now he wanted it, wanted freedom from the unrelenting aches that ran up his torso and scoured his mind.

He drifted through time and space, unaware. Once he heard a noise and found Hoffmeister staring at him again, worry etched in him. The next time he awakened he stared up into the mocking eyes of Sergeant Major Vernon Wiltz, and something pierced through his weary oblivion and brought him to the stark edge of terror.

"You're a slow learner, Toole."

Santiago didn't respond. He collected himself to yell if he must.

"The guard said you'd returned to the world of the living.

Too bad. What did you do it for, Toole? Wasn't a doctor's income enough? Graft. A pity. Ruint your career. Some lawmen just ain't above temptation. We had to report it, of course, how you and them merchants stole from the army, and how you almost—you got in a good lick, Toole. Surprised me. I thought you were some tiddlywink. Got me in the lights. I never forget. I always get even. I ain't even yet. Know that? Ain't even. Someone gets me in the lights, and we're never even.''

Santiago couldn't think of anything to say. The sergeant major loomed over him like a bear, all teeth and muscle and awesome claws that could smash his faltering life away with one smack.

"You look a little beat, Toole. I don't think you'll ever get well. I read that chart on you. My boys didn't like no grafter sheriff holding a gun to them, so they said their piece with their boots and fists. Too bad you lived, Toole.''

Wiltz loomed over the cot, his hands opening and closing, his feral eyes revealing how deeply he relished this total power.

Santiago braced himself for fiery pain and yelled, a long, hoarse howl that erupted wolflike from his esophagus and echoed out into the gloomy hall. He howled again, feeling vicious pain lance him. He howled, howled, like a man demented.

An orderly burst in, and then another, staring at the sheriff in the iron army cot, and then at Wiltz.

The sergeant major watched them boil in, eyed Toole, and laughed easily, a fine happy chortle that yanked the orderlies to a sudden halt.

"Very good, Toole," Wiltz said. "Very good," and wandered out of the room.

Chapter 11

Sergeant Major Wiltz had stopped it and Mimi never understood why. She'd writhed on her bed, her own sacrosanct place, while some rank corporal yanked her skirts high, and then Wiltz had appeared.

"No," he said.

"She's a squaw. Toole's squaw."

"You heard me."

Nothing changed. The man pawed her, ripped at her things. She scratched and bit. Then Wiltz's massive paw knocked him off, sent him sprawling to the rug.

"Goddammit, Sarge. . . ."

"We'll do things the army way."

She stared wildly up at him, watching blood leak from his armpit and stain his blouse. The corporal picked himself slowly off her rug, grunting in pain. Two others stared.

"We don't doodle sheriff's wives, do we, breed lady? It don't look good."

Wiltz's blood slid down his blouse to his waist, but he ignored it. He looked gray. They left her then, vanishing from Santiago's home and office. She lay paralyzed on her bed, her skirts still bunched at her waist, quaking and confused. They'd come back! They'd kill her. They'd . . . Santiago, oh, Santiago, dead on the street, his body convulsing in its death throes from a beating beyond comprehension. Tears wouldn't come. Only terror. Santiago dead. Sheriff, doctor, pounded and kicked dead. . . . Blue-shirted killers, killers of her mother's people, killers of women and children and boys of all the tribes, killers of Santiago.

She lay moribund, rigid, suffocated, dreading a world beyond her dark door so terrifying she dared not pierce into the daylight beyond. Her heart stilled and grief replaced terror. She'd not been assaulted, but close, so close. She felt violated anyway, her woman's weakness open and helpless. Penetrated, although she hadn't been. Naked, although they'd seen only her bronzed thighs. Raped by intent if not violent will.

She lay there whole, almost, but Santiago . . . gone from her arms. She saw the shape of things. A breed in Milestown without Santiago. Walk Main Street and be shunned, a breed rather than Santiago's wife. Merchants who'd been civil . . . would be curt. No place for the likes of you here, their manner would say. And when a priest showed up on his rounds and said the Mass, they'd wall her out. Oh, Santiago. Oh, Jesu, Jesu, Santiago. . . .

She needed to see him. Hold his hand. Nerve herself for the pulp of his face and ruin of his slim body. She pulled herself up, sat on the edge of her bed, preparing herself for the frosted world beyond. Bury Santiago. She walked to the front door and peered out into sunlight. Her magpie flapped off the picket fence. She straightened her yellow skirts and stepped out, down the narrow path trodden to dust by the ill, the hurt, the frightened and victimized. She rounded the corner to Main, looking for Santiago. Looking to say good-bye, steeling herself. No soldiers remained; no heap of army goods. Main Street lay deserted and quiet in the sun. No Santiago. They'd taken his body away. They'd wrap it in linen and lay it in a sepulchre and the women would weep. She wondered why she thought of Jesus. They'd crucified Santiago and taken him away. Maybe to Sylvane's, where they might let a widow weep. . . .

She edged frightened along the wide street, past the meat market and Huffman's photographic studio with its portraits of Sioux chiefs in the window, to the place where Santiago fell. Nothing there, except small drops of blood to tell a story. She stood friendless in the sun and then fled, smitten by some evil rising from Milestown, not knowing where she went or why, only that she had to flee.

Two hours later she stumbled into Two Moons' village up the Tongue, where the Cheyenne awaited their fate with more patience and resignation than the army had any right to expect. They stared at her, the doctor's wife with the ghosts in her and wild eyes, and followed silently as she wove her way to Two Moons' own lodge. His young wives said nothing, reading something in her eyes, and drew her inside the lodge, and covered her with a fine robe even though the day had turned hot. There she quaked, and there White Antelope and Sees the Dawn learned her story, and whispered it among the People.

There she stayed, the guest of the young chief himself, but she scarcely knew the passage of time or the setting of suns. Santiago dead. She saw Santiago in the dawn and dusk, in the eyes of the calm, in the soul of the medicine man who watched her sharply. She saw Santiago in the Morning Star and in the withered grass and in the naked bronze boys playing on the river bank. Until they brought her news that Santiago hovered at the edge of life, in a coma, in the fort infirmary. Santiago alive, barely, wounded unto the edge of eternal darkness. She wept. Rejoiced. Despaired. Raged. Grew sullen, and sharpened her hate. She'd never known hate, but now it blossomed like an orchid in her, and she nursed it and watered it and let it run down her limbs to her fingers and toes, until her body hated as much as her soul did.

Then came more news at last: Santiago had awakened from his long sleep. The orderlies themselves had said it, when the Cheyenne women had come to clean in exchange for waste foods from the hospital mess. And gossip.

Alive, but under a cloud. Dishonored. This part of it they hadn't understood, except that a guard stood at Santiago's door all day and into the evening. Not to protect him, but to keep him prisoner.

Two Moons' wives smiled.

"I must see Santiago," Mimi said.

They clapped hands to mouths, but their dark eyes shone.

Late that night, when the Big Dipper had spun far around the North Star, she slipped into her washed and mended yellow dress and out into the soft August night, hearing the crickets and the rhythms of night things. A small breeze toyed with her.

She might have dressed in squaw calicos and skins, but chose her white woman's clothing instead. The guard might shoot a squaw; a white woman might be an officer's wife. She walked, afraid and eager, up the dusty, manure-laden path northward toward Fort Keogh, under a friendly heaven. Santiago. Were you really there, alive? She felt ashamed that she'd fled Milestown—an act of cowardice and terror and hysteria. No. She'd find courage now. Impulsively she blessed herself, her hand flying from her head to her breast: in the name of the Father, the Son, and the Holy Spirit. Amen. Santiago. I will kiss every wound and heal it with my touch. I will hold your hand and see the light in your eyes, even if your room is thick with night. I will lift my heart to you and tell you that I am well and not to worry. I will heal you and you will heal me, and I will tell you how ashamed I am that I fled. Dead. You were dead and I had no place, no place. . . .

The Fort hulked like a river cliff, with moonlight filtering between buildings, patching the grass with cold. There would be guards, but she'd ignore them. She walked boldly toward the infirmary, a place she'd been in several times with Santiago—Dr. Toole—at open houses, during visits, among officers and gentlemen. She walked boldly along the front of officers' row, where those officers and gentlemen and their ladies slept the sleep of the innocent. Clapboard, some of them. Others rising, of dun brick with broad, comfortable verandas and mansard roofs. No one said nay, no challenge erupted from the moon-shadows. No lamp glowed in the infirmary. No attendants whiled the night away. And no lock barred the door when she swung it open and entered a place redolent with acrid odors, carbolic stabbing her nostrils, and fainter, sinister smells. White light lanced from gleaming windows. A man coughed. She felt eyes on her. A dozen fevered eyes. She stood, gathering her wits and fighting an instinct to turn away and stop this foolishness. She had, after all, only gossip filtered fourth-hand down to the village of Cheyenne, miles up the Tongue.

A reception area with a woodstove and desk. Beyond, a central corridor, wards on either side. Would she have to peer into each iron cot, poke anyone whose head lay buried in a pillow, risk uproar? Foolish woman. Turn and leave at once. But Mimi had learned hate and her will had stiffened to iron. And she loved, loved Santiago as she never had before. She peered into moonstreaked wards on either side and then walked boldly to the rear. Two closed doors. She tried the one on the moonlit side, opening it swiftly and wincing at its shriek. Within, a bandaged man jerked up, gasping at his own pain.

"Santo!" she cried.

"Mimi?"

She heard his unnatural breathing, the rasp of air from wounded lungs.

She plunged to him, the image of him rubbery in the wet lenses of her eyes. He winced when she touched him, but she felt one hand, his right hand, touch her, fingers finding her shoulder and cheek and lips and breast.

"I thought you were dead!" she whispered.

"I was," he said. "Where . . . ?"

"Two Moons' lodge. Weeping days away, Santo."

"Holy Mary."

"How are you hurt, Santo? Where? I will heal you with kisses; *Jesu Dominie*, I will heal you."

He catalogued his wounds for her until she could bear no more. She found space on his narrow cot and nestled herself beside him, not speaking for minutes, but telling him all the things between man and woman ever witnessed by stars and moon.

"I've got to get out of here," he whispered.

"But Santo . . ."

"Soon. I need your help. I need some things, Mimi."

She listened, frightened and fierce.

Januarius Quigby had never seen a man as formidable as the sergeant major who guarded the post HQ like a sphinx. The man dwarfed the reception room, turned the desk before him into dollhouse furniture, and radiated menace like a powder magazine with a lit fuse. He even terrorized the walls. For the first time in his career Quigby felt real dread. The sergeant major's feral eyes surveyed Quigby and dismissed him, as if he were a dead mouse being carried by the tail to the nearest ditch.

"Ah! Er . . . perhaps you can help me," Quigby muttered, his soft jowls vibrating with anxiety. "I'm a representative, sir—"

"Quartermaster's south end of fort, west of parade, office in warehouse," said Wiltz.

"I don't, I don't . . . I'm . . . interested in direct sales. The men. Most of my line is personal goods. . . ."

"Well, what is it? What do you want?"

"Permission. Um, to approach . . . Would your CO permit a sales representative of a medical and apothecary line, plus other things, ah, magazines. Household things for the ladies on suds row . . ."

Wiltz yawned. "Talk to the post surgeon. Three buildings south, this side of the parade."

"I will, I will. You wouldn't be interested in . . . ah . . . aids and comforts to manhood. Cures for male diseases."

Something lit up in the sergeant major's eyes, something like raffish humor. "Whatcha got, drummerboy?"

Something relaxed in Quigby's mind. It always did when the barb caught. "Why, Sergeant, my most popular and proven items are things men don't readily discuss much, and can't be advertised for obvious reasons, and that's why these products can reach markets only by the candidness of sales representatives. You see, I'm an agent of the famed apothecary company, Gore and Son. Bethlehem, Pennsylvania. You've heard of them, of course. Seen their pharmacopoeia in every hospital and doctor's office worldwide. . . .

"Well, Sergeant, we have two outstanding products. One, called Derrick Tonic, helps . . . ah . . . helps a man debilitated and unable to rise to the occasion, heh, heh, ah. . . ."

Quigby waited for the sergeant to react to his little joke, but unaccountably the man simply stared, blank as a wall.

"At any rate, Derrick contains draughts of a secret ingredient discovered recently by anthropologists examining the tips of blow-gun arrows of Amazon natives—and shipped at great expense to Gore and Son—"

Wiltz yawned.

"Now my other product is a cream, a salve, with another of Gore and Son's great medical breakthroughs, a means to cure certain cankers and discharges. . . . In short, a means to perfect comfort and health in four days. In particularly bad cases an extra day might be required, and once I heard of two more days, almost a week before blessed relief. But rare, of course. . . ."

"How much?"

"Derrick is two dollars the bottle; the salve, called Gore's Salvation, is three dollars the jar, and will last sufficient for the cure. Now that's expensive for, ah, enlisted men, but well within the means of officers, commissioned and otherwise."

"Too much."

"Guaranteed, sir. Money back. Just refund the bottle—a few pennies for postage will get your money back, no questions asked. A senior man like yourself could afford it."

Wiltz leered, as Quigby had expected. "Not interested, but you might try the noncom officers' barracks. And suds row. Yes, especially suds row. Talk to the wives."

"Then, sir, I have permission to discuss these things here? I need that, sir. The privacy. I can't very well sell a gross to the quartermaster, can I?"

Wiltz leered again and rubbed his skull.

"Find Sergeant Buford. He'll buy the Derrick. Try Clete Horn and Max Liggett. Single corporals. Tell them I sent you. Vernon Wiltz. Tell them I insist on it. And over on the Row, you just have a little chat with LeMat and Polanc and their ladies. Try them ladies first. They're the ones get the good of it."

Quigby exulted. "Thanks, Mister! I'd just like to leave a sample, whichever you wish, as a little thank you. . . ."

Wiltz chuckled. "Leave some Derrick for the CO. I'll put it on his desk."

"Deeelighted!" Quigby exclaimed, digging into his ashes-of-roses carpetbag for his sample bottles.

Moments later, Quigby was trotting across the parade to the barracks and hunting up the noncom quarters. Everything had gone perfectly. Men responded that way, most of them. Amusement. A chance for a practical joke. They rarely bought, but they often sent Quigby to hunt someone else down. Just as Wiltz had. Ah . . . that was a man, that Wiltz, a catamount in blues.

He found the noncoms' quarters easily; he had an eye for the ways of the world. They all had private rooms, unlike the enlisted men in their barracks. Silent now in the middle of the day, and yet some would be around, the ones on night duty. . . . He poked through echoing hallways, assaulted by mustard-colored pine and the rancid odor of unwashed bodies and urine from the sinks in the outhouses to the rear.

He paused suddenly, aware that he should study the place, note its exits, its open windows, the clutter of private possessions heaped on hardwood floors and shelves and tables. He peered through an open door, spotted a man snoring, wrapped loosely in a sheet. A blue blouse with corporal's stripes hung over a bentwood chair.

No name. But it didn't matter. Before the sun set today, he'd know the looks of each noncom fingered by Sapp, the man's quarters, his whereabouts, his habits, his family if he had one, his duty hours . . . and probable ways the man could meet with accident or illness or the Hand of God.

In the far left room he found a man, shirtless, sitting on his cot and blacking his boots. A hairy man. This one looked like a gorilla, in fact. Januarius Quigby had no chest hair at all, and his chubby form was as hairless and pink as a baby's. Hairy men fascinated him. And this brute in particular, whose back was matted with black fur, as well as chest and arms and the back of his hands, and whatever furry coat lay beneath the belt of his blue britches. The man could be skinned for a beaver coat.

"Ahem . . ."

The man looked up from his blacking and surveyed a drummer, his gaze sliding from pudgy face to fat fingers clutching his carpetbag.

"You selling something?"

"Why, yes. Sergeant Wiltz—Vernon Wiltz—suggested I come here. He thought you might wish to order some of my products. I have a famous line of apothecary goods, Gore and Son; you've heard of them of course. . . . I'm Quigby, Januarius. And what is yours?"

"Wiltz sent you, eh? I'm Chet Buford. Show me whatcha got, Quigby."

Ten minutes later, to Quigby's mild surprise, Buford ordered a jar of Gore's Salvation. Januarius wrote up the order assiduously. When the jar arrived, Buford would no longer be among the living, but that was just the point. Just the point. Every order that Quigby took got filled promptly.

"That's a lot of money out of a sergeant's pay," Buford said dourly, digging in his purse.

"I wish it could be cheaper, Sergeant. I wish enlisted men could afford it, too. But remember, money-back guarantee."

"Yeah, sure. Now where do I rub this stuff?"

"Just follow the directions, right on the jar. You write me when it works. I collect testimonials. Right there on the sales slip. That's my address, right there. . . . Anyone else I could visit with here?"

"Try after six," Buford said. "If this damn stuff doesn't work . . ."

"Who's that asleep down the hall?"

"Liggett. He's got night duty."

"Does he, ah, have problems?"

"Yeah, the opposite kind!" Buford guffawed.

"Oh! That's funny!" said Quigby. He'd heard it fifty times. They all knew someone who had the opposite problem. Maybe he should bottle up some Gore's Anti-Derrick and try it.

Through the rest of that day the small, porky drummer with fat fingers traipsed invisibly across Fort Keogh, from barracks to drill field to infirmary—where he got a look at Corporal LeMat standing guard—to suds row, for amiable and discreet chats with Corporal and Mrs. Polanc, and the LeMat woman, who turned beet-red and shooed him off. That left Cletus Horn. Some casual inquiry revealed that Corporal Horn had no assigned duties and was waiting out a month to see if he might recover the use of an injured arm. If not, the army would be done with him. He tracked Horn down in the Fifth Infantry library and reading room, a remarkable place for an isolated post.

"Yeah," said Horn. "Bottle of both if you promise delivery in three weeks. Ah'm gonna muster out with a month of joy in my pockets."

Januarius Quigby wrote out the order, which he promised to

wire to Denver City, and in the process found out what he needed to know, such as the date of Horn's probable discharge. He liked Horn, and that disturbed him. It seemed unjust to dispatch a man who'd be gone in a few days, a man who'd paid a heavy price. . . .

Late in the day Quigby turned his hack back toward Miles, his mind content and idly pondering ways and means.

Chapter 12

Toole woke up mean. His fever raged; his head throbbed; every busted bone and laceration bit at him and fueled the rage building up in him like a plugged volcano. He snarled at the orderly who brought him breakfast, and lay poised on his cot to tongue-lash the next mortal who appeared in his door. His Irish was up, and he didn't care who knew it or what consequences it might bring.

He'd wormed Mimi's story from her: the attempted assault on her; the ransacking of his office; the theft of every bit of evidence he'd collected. He'd nail them; he'd take on the whole U.S. Army and anyone else who laid hand to Mimi and tampered with evidence. He'd get them or die trying. The feeling bubbled like lava in the crucible of his soul, until the fever of it seared his body.

That was how Colonel Orville Wade found him. The commanding officer paused at the door, stared at the fevered sheriff wallowing in the iron cot, and looked faintly startled.

"Hoffmeister told me . . . that you're better. Able to discuss matters," he said.

Toole knew how he must look: stubble-jawed and hollow-eyed, with heat daggering from his eyes. He'd scarcely slept after Mimi had slid out, and the rest of the night had been a tumbling jumble of pain, rage, and drastic night schemes to right howling wrongs.

"I'll discuss them all right, Wade."

The colonel paused, bitten by Toole's savagery.

"I want your version. I have everyone else's," Wade said,

112

pushing in and settling himself in a bentwood chair near the cot.

"The better to hang me with," Toole shot at him.

Wade pursed his lips, looking pained. "You're in trouble, Toole. Resisting an army dragnet. Kicking a sergeant and brawling with our men. Telling merchants to retrieve confiscated goods. I hear maybe you're in with them. Graft."

"Is that the charge? Graft?" Santiago snarled. "You believe it, of course. The army takes care of its own."

Wade's face flared red. "Listen here, Toole. I don't like your attitude. You're lucky to be alive. You're protecting crooks, that's obvious. Oh, the merchants have all come over to tell me what a good man you are, but it's obvious what you've been up to."

"Is it now!" Toole snapped. "I suppose telling Gatz to pick up some confiscated revolvers, all civilian nickel-plate with ivory grips, is graft? And telling him to write their serial numbers and give them to you to check against your army lists is graft?"

He watched Wade's pupils contract and his mustache twitch.

"And I suppose protecting my wife from detainment and assault by your goons is graft," he snarled.

"You're bucking the Army, Toole."

"I'm bucking the Army, yes. I'm hunting down a party of army killers you're protecting. I'm going to nail them for stealing evidence, Wade. They took evidence I'd collected at the Hogtown site. Obstructing justice is a criminal offense. Go run your own dragnet of the noncom barracks. If they're as dumb as I hope, you'll find some spent bullets and a revolver with the grips burnt away—the one that shot Horn. Probably in Wiltz's room."

"Horn? What are you talking about, Toole?"

"The Hogtown weapon that put a bullet into Horn's arm. Check the hospital records. Right here. He was admitted the night Hogtown burned—allegedly having shot himself cleaning his revolver—at one or two in the morning."

"That's not evidence, Toole."

"Not for you. For me it is. Let me tell you something, Wade. I'm going to get those killers. I'm going to get you, if you don't cooperate. When it comes to an Irish sheriff against your army, your army will lose. Unless you kill me first."

Wade looked startled, and Toole found savage pleasure in it.

"I'm coming out of this bed and when I do, Wade, you'll never know what hit you."

The commanding officer laughed shortly. "Fever's turned you mad," he said. "I'll move you to the guardhouse and then we'll see about wild threats."

"What charges?"

Wade's pupils went small again. "None yet. But there'll be enough. The army doesn't need any out here."

"It's too late, Wade. A guardhouse won't silence me."

Wade looked pained again, and impatient. "I didn't come here to get into a shouting match. I thought you'd like to explain your conduct. I'm a reasonable and fair-minded man. An officer must be, or fail his duty."

"Get out of here!" Toole yelled. An orderly appeared in the door and then vanished.

Wade sighed primly. "Very well. I'll discuss your conduct in my notes. I have excellent notes. And the sergeant major's exhaustive report. And goods taken from town, inventoried at over two thousand. From the crooks who think so highly of you."

"Did Wiltz record where they came from, by merchant?"

"No. He just listed it all—blankets, arms, everything."

"So the innocent and guilty are lumped together. Saloon-keepers who took anything for a drink; parlorhouse women who traded for what they could get, all lumped in with good merchants like Hjorts Gatz."

"Perfectly unnecessary," Wade said. "That whole village lives like a parasite off the post."

"I thought you kept careful records," Toole jeered. "I thought you were interested in justice, guilt, innocence. But you didn't think to ask the sergeant major. Everyone in Milestown's guilty. Oh, that'll look good for army examiners."

Wade stood stiffly and started to leave.

"One thing, Wade," Santiago snapped. The colonel stopped at the door. "If you cover up murder, you're an accessory to the crime. That'll look nice on your army record. Now get out of my room. Go perfume your armpits, Colonel. You sweat too much.''

A thunderous scowl flashed across Wade's blood-gorged face as he wheeled out of the room.

Santiago glared at the retreating form. He'd become so mad he'd forgotten his own pain for a few moments. They'd probably kill him. He'd threatened the commanding officer of Fort Keogh. He wished Colonel Miles were around. He'd like to take a bite out of the Fifth Infantry commander as well. He sat poised on his cot, angry beyond pain, waiting to pounce, when Hoffmeister appeared.

"Gott Almighty, Santiago."

"Get me out of here!''

"Everything I heard. Your voice—it rattled in the wards. Everyone hears.''

"Good! No secrets that way.''

Hoffmeister grabbed Toole's wrist and took the pulse, frowning.

"Over a hundred, Santiago.''

But even as he pronounced it Toole felt his tension start to loosen inside of him, the tightness of rage sliding away.

"I'll be all right, Adelbert. Now are you going to help me?''

"It'd kill you to move you. . . That lung . . .''

"Then put me in the middle of a ward. I want witnesses.''

Hoffmeister shrugged. "I am ordered to keep you here. But maybe I can do something.''

"Not if they haul me to the guardhouse.''

"I won't allow that. It'd kill you.''

"That's what Wade has in mind, along with about six non-coms who think I know too much.''

Dr. Hoffmeister poured a spoonful of liquid from a familiar blue-glass, square-shaped bottle.

"I don't want that.''

"You take it." Hoffmeister lifted the spoon to Santiago's still swollen mouth. "You need it. Calm is what you need. Slow down.''

Wearily Toole agreed. They'd probably slaughter him in his sleep, but he needed the laudanum now. His body was laboring and howling under the pressure of rage. He opened his mouth slightly, feeling the lancing hurt of his cracked jaw, and swallowed.

"Ach! You're a bad patient. Doctors make bad patients."

"I took it, didn't I?"

Hoffmeister nodded, corked the bottle, and replaced it in a satchel he carried on his rounds. "I will think of something."

Holy Mary, how it floated him. He settled back on his pillow as the opiate feathered away his pain and anger both. His mind clarified and became piercing and bright, like his father's. He turned his new, keen mind to the problem before him. Killers to track down; justice obstructed; evidence destroyed; army resisting if not covering up. Trapped by injury in a cot at the Fort. Grave injury, too dizzy and weak even to sit up, and in danger of relapse if he tried to escape. Trapped, and in danger. . . .

His mind seemed charged with lucidity and excitement. Well, then, create an opportunity from it all. Was he not in the lair of those he hoped to indict? If he couldn't leave his bed to pursue them, might he not bring them to his bed and collect evidence from them, one way or another? The thought galvanized him. Bring them one by one to his hospital room and interview them. He had allies now. Mimi at least, and maybe Hoffmeister. Mimi could bring him the things he might need—indeed, when she returned she'd have some of them in her reticule. And Adelbert, too. Turn the tables! They thought they had him here, immobilized, unable to do anything more about the Hogtown killings. But he'd fool them. They'd see him lying helpless and talk carelessly, especially if he plied them with a few tongue looseners. And if good bourbon didn't work, some other things might. The tools of the trade a sheriff used daily. Santiago closed his eyes, saw red flecks dancing across a black ground, and laughed.

An uproar down the corridor plucked him out of his opalescent dreaming. Mimi. He peered around, orienting himself to long shadows and low sun. Late afternoon? Or early morning? It panicked him that he might have drifted through an entire night.

"You can't see him, ma'am. Ah have orders not to let—"

Horn's voice. Cletus Horn on guard out at the reception area.

"I'm his wife," Mimi snapped. "I brought things. A nightshirt. His robe, some slippers. If you stop me I'm going to go straight to Colonel—"

"Sorry, Mizz Toole, Ah got my—"

"Corporal!" Hoffmeister's gruff snarl. "This is Mrs. Toole. Dr. Toole's wife. Now you just let her by, or I'll wring your neck."

"Ah have to follow orders, suh. Colonel Wade, he's afraid some town merchants'll kidnap the sheriff, haul him plumb out of here, and he says I'm to stop—"

"Corporal"—Hoffmeister's voice turned withering—"does Mrs. Toole look like she's about to kidnap him? She knows better than anyone that moving him might kill him. If you want, I'll go tell Colonel Wade you're detaining her."

Santiago heard a muffled sound and staccato steps on the plank floor, and then Mimi burst in, staggering under a load. Her own reticule tucked under her arm, a portmanteau of his, and his pigskin medical valise. Her golden flesh glowed with the anger she exuded. His eyes devoured her, as if she were an angel descended from above, in her white dimity and black choker, and soft, wavy, jet hair—a gift from her father—loose about her oval face.

"Santo! That idiot corporal wouldn't—Oh, Santo! You look terrible. How are you?"

She dumped her burdens beside the cot and slid onto it, kissing him. He felt her soft kiss and pain where her lips touched his swollen and scabbed face. "I brought everything you asked," she whispered. "I found everything, even the Starr. It's at the bottom of your valise."

His Remington had vanished in the scuffle, a prize of war for some one of his assailants. But he'd confiscated a Starr from a disorderly and drunk buffalo-runner a few days earlier.

"I have mine, too. In my bag," she added.

He heard a clearing of throat at the door. Adelbert.

"You surprised me, Mrs. Toole," the doctor said discreetly.

She looked into Santiago's eyes, and then turned to the post surgeon. "I did what I had to. I left town for a while," she said quietly.

Santiago detected a bitter irony in her voice that probably eluded Hoffmeister.

"I am at home now. And will be visiting here," she added, squeezing Santiago's good hand. "I brought him some comforts."

Indeed she did, he thought. Comforts.

"Was that Corporal Horn, Adelbert?"

The surgeon nodded. "Wade's got him on light duty. He's still not well and his left arm won't work, but a four to midnight shift out at that desk won't hurt him."

The news delighted Santiago. Horn. Corporal Horn, soon to be discharged. A man whose loyalties to his noncom peers ebbed each day. An ex-Confederate, too. A place to start, a wedge. Maybe a battered sheriff could track down murder from a hospital cot.

"Tell Horn I'd enjoy a visit," he said. "I'm getting strong enough to see some visitors."

"Don't push it," Hoffmeister muttered. "I won't even ask what you've got in your physician's valise, or what powders and draughts you'll be giving yourself. Only keep me informed. I've never had a stubborn Irish doctor under my care. Ach, you'll try everything before your body's half able."

Santiago Toole smiled, and squeezed Mimi's fierce hand.

Hoffmeister left them to themselves, and instantly Mimi's hands found him and caressed him, touching each injury, finding hurts and gently pressing against them while she muttered incantations in Assiniboin, Latin, French, extracting medicine from everything that had been her world. He laughed, enjoying the slide of her fingers, the intimacy of them and the love exuding from them, and her fierce muttering. Then at last she blessed him, her hand bladed like a priest's, the swift cruciform shape almost hanging in the air behind her arm.

She stayed an hour until his wounds crabbed at him again, and then kissed him adieu, promising to return in the morning.

"Be careful, Mimi," he whispered. "We're both so vulnerable."

She rattled her reticule at him, muttering imprecations and clutching at her small weapon through its cloth.

"On your way out, tell Corporal Horn I'd enjoy visiting.

And—oh, Mimi. Could you please wash those things?'' He pointed at his battered, bloodied shirt, vest, and trousers hanging from a wall peg. ''But leave the star. In fact, I'd like it pinned to my robe.''

These things she did and left, and a while later Cletus Horn wandered in.

''You wanted me, doctah?''

''A little talk, Corporal.''

The man seated himself in the bentwood chair, half curious, half bored. Santiago decided not to mince words, even if it meant more risk. The man could kill him with no great difficulty.

''How's your arm? Can you use your fingers at all?''

Horn shook his head.

''An expensive price for that raid on Hogtown. You'd planned a career in the army, and now you're on your way out and facing a tough civilian life, too.''

Horn looked startled, and then hid his thoughts behind a stony mask.

''Perhaps you're forgetting I'm sheriff of Custer County and I've been collecting evidence. A lot of it, Horn. You shot that Hogtown kid, Herold somebody, poxy-faced. Got him at least three times. I found the mangled lead. Found the revolver he used to shoot you, right where it landed when his hand flew out.'' He waited for that to register, seeing fear and iron in Horn's eyes.

''Oh, that's not all, Horn. There's a living witness. I've already told Wiltz that but he doesn't believe me. Your partners in crime ransacked my office, took evidence. You're lucky you weren't there because that's a crime itself—put a man up for years. So, Horn, I'm closing in. Laid up here a while, but that doesn't mean my investigation's stopped or that your little party of noncoms will escape murder warrants and probable hanging. I don't think the army can protect you, once the evidence is made public. A lot of it has been, of course. Written out and sent along to territorial authorities. It went out with today's mail dispatch, so your bunch is pretty naked just now. . . . And it's too late, Horn. Too late to kill Sheriff Toole.''

"Ah don't know what you're raving about."

Santiago smiled, feeling the scabs of his facial wounds crinkle.

"Of course you're leaving soon, chance to get away before it all falls on you—start a new life, free of this mess. You must be wondering how you ever got involved with that bunch of noncom toughs. Especially Wiltz. Must have been hard to say no to a man like that, who could make or break you with a snap of his fingers."

"Ah don't have to listen to this nonsense, Toole."

"No, you can go back out and brood, maybe sneak back here, put a bullet into me. Get discharged and politely disappear in this giant western wilderness. Always looking behind you, Horn, to see who's coming down the trail with a warrant in his pocket. Like me. Like the next sheriff who sees your mug on a Wanted dodger. You want that?"

Horn stared silently at him, hard agate eyes alert. He glanced at the doorway, looking for eavesdroppers.

"You don't owe Wiltz and his noncoms anything. He got you into trouble, wrecked your arm and career, and now you're almost out of it. Maybe I could help you get out and away, scot-free, lad, if you'd trade that for a few things."

Santiago said nothing for a while, watching Horn absorb all that.

"You're full of it, Sheriff. You ain't got a witness and you're just trying to trap me, pin something on me Ah didn't do."

"Well, you can take your chances in court, then. You think on it, Corporal. Wiltz got you into this. Now he's digging a hole for himself and the others. Tampering with my evidence. Lying to Colonel Wade. You know, of course, that Wade's been told what really happened there. He's afraid of Wiltz, that's plain. But he's also afraid of getting himself into big trouble and wrecking his own career.

"Just like you, Horn—sitting right on the edge and not knowing which way to jump. You're in better shape than the rest, Horn. No one is going to worry much about shooting that poxy killer, even if you shot him asleep. And you don't have to worry about being charged with tampering with evidence, resisting arrest by lawful authority, or covering up a crime. I figure you'll walk out of this—if you give me reasons to let you go."

Corporal Horn laughed harshly. "You done with your palaver?" he demanded.

"No, Horn, I'm not. You're under arrest. You leave Custer County now, and I'll put fugitive papers on you."

Horn wheezed at him. "Some talk from a half-daid man," he said, stalking out.

Santiago watched him go, wondering how it would turn out.

Chapter 13

The gossip startled Sergeant Major Vernon Wiltz. It emanated from the cavalry contingent and sifted its way over to infantry, officer to officer, and then down to the man who guarded the portals of the office of the commanding officer, the man who really ran Fort Keogh.

Cavalry Lieutenant Valor Benedict had been running his personal mare up the river, keeping her fit and fine under saddle, when before him rose an amazing apparition: a large edifice of board and batten, well along, being nailed together by a small army of foreigners. Not exactly on the site of the late and unlamented Hogtown, but nearby, a hundred yards or so south of the river trail, where the Northern Pacific would soon run. The exact purpose of this long rectangle, and a small cottage rising behind it, was unknown, but Lieutenant Benedict suspected the worst. A commercial building obviously—and the commerce would be Fort Keogh's.

"I think, sah, I will investigate," Wiltz announced to Colonel Wade.

"Send out a small party," Wade replied.

"I think I'd like to examine this personally, sah. It may involve the army."

Wade stared testily. "I don't want another incident."

Wiltz shrugged. "It'd be a good idea, sah, to find out who owns it and what the building's for."

"It's off the military reservation, Sergeant. I'd rather you didn't."

"I'm the soul of discretion, sah."

"I'm not so sure you are. I've been dealing with unhappy merchants in Milestown. So far, I've kept their complaints to myself and off your record. See that it stays that way. I trust you understand me, Wiltz."

"Perfectly, sah. I'll report before nightfall."

He walked out onto the parade, amused. Whatever was written on his record was what he chose to place there. Things got lost. The new building puzzled him. Not Sapp. Dead and a thousand miles down the river. Probably another den, fancier this time, but intended to suck the army dry, the way Hogtown had. Another dive to sicken his enlisted men, weaken their morale, poison them with rotgut, and steal everything at the Fort that wasn't nailed down and padlocked. He'd find out who, and deal with it.

He found Cletus Horn in the Fifth Infantry reading room, and Max Liggett, requisitioned three cavalry mounts, and rode west. No enlisted men. This would be another noncom party; a reconnoiter first, followed by some swift and decisive action.

"Another dump," he said to Horn. "That's what I figure. Looks like we'll have a little party again."

Horn looked annoyed. "Ah don't know why you roped me in. Ah'll be out of the army in a couple of weeks."

"You're still in and still under orders, Corporal." Something in Horn's tone graveled Wiltz. If Horn was turning coward on him, he'd damn well fix the bastard; maybe keep him in another six months, maybe give him a little new shooting to do with his good arm.

"Maybe it's just a warehouse or something for the railroad when it comes," ventured Liggett.

"Well now, Liggett, how will we know unless we look?"

Liggett kept silent, and the three of them rode quietly through an August day toward Hogtown. It had turned dry, and dun grass looked ready to burn at the toss of a careless cigar. Which set Vernon Wiltz to thinking. Maybe some subtlety this time . . . A grass fire.

Meanwhile he wanted to know who owned the land, if anyone. Had Sapp owned his or just squatted? Probably railroad land, so close to the right of way. Who, then?

He hated horses, and this one hated him. It walked sullenly

forward, dragging along behind Horn's and Liggett's mounts. His two hundred sixty pounds was well over a hundred more than any good cavalryman's, and the horse knew it. He kicked the horse uneasily, feeling the animal stiffen and its spine arch. But it didn't buck. Wiltz prided himself on fearing nothing, but an unruly horse came closest to alarming him. He always figured if it came down to it, he'd pull a horse's head off and bust its neck before he'd let it run away with him or buck him off.

They heard the staccato of hammers before they rounded the last shoulder of bluff, and the rhythmic rasp of saws as they drew close. And then they beheld it, an astonishing thing, a framed building of new white wood still bleeding yellow sap, and a whole army, men and boys, swarming over it.

Wiltz reined up and stared. Foreigners, babbling in some strange tongue, hammering roof planks down and nailing battens over the cracks in the side walls. A good hundred feet long, this place, and forty wide, and some small building behind it. A false front on the river side, shallow peak behind it. A mountain of sawn lumber. Beyond, on a flat near the burnt corpse of Hogtown, a tent city; women tending cookfires, children dutifully at work carrying wood and nails, water and food.

"It don't look like no dive," Liggett muttered. "Like maybe their church or something. Meeting hall or something."

"We'll see," Wiltz snapped. They'd been spotted now, and workmen stared at the three mounted noncoms. But the hammering and sawing never slowed. These men seemed almost feverish with haste, and at the same time taking some pride in their work. As little as Wiltz knew of construction, he could see order and care in all this. He touched heels to his mount and yanked its head around savagely. Behind him, Horn and Liggett followed.

"Hey! What's this? What's happening here?" he yelled at the nearest workman. The man smiled blankly and shrugged.

Several spoke to him in a strange tongue, which peeved him.

"Who the hell speaks American?" he bellowed. He'd gotten a few of these dillies in the army and he'd learned that the best way to deal with them was to shout. They might not understand the words but they understood the shouting. He yelled a few more times, and watched them mutter to each other. Off at the tents, the women looked alarmed and slid out of sight.

At last a gaunt man with hollow cheeks and silver-rimmed round spectacles clambered down from a roof.

"Ja?" he asked. "I speak a little."

"Who are you?" Wiltz snapped, feeling his mount shift under him.

The man looked frightened. "Ole Tollefson, Herr Sergeant."

"You them Norwegians from up the river?"

Tollefson faltered, tugging at his britches. "That is us, Herr Sergeant."

"What the hell are you doing here?"

"We are employed to build this place."

"Who's hiring you. What is this dump?"

"This is I believe a dance hall and a saloon."

"I asked you who hired you, Tollefson."

"Uffdah! It was a man named Quigby."

The name seemed vaguely familiar to Wiltz, but he couldn't place it. "Describe him," he snapped.

"Very large, Herr. Very grand."

"What do you mean by that?"

"Fat. Fleshy. With a gold coin on his head. Dressed fine, a gentleman's suit."

"Gold on his head? Where can I find him, Tollefson?"

The man shrugged. "Sometimes he comes in the night to see. I suppose maybe he stays in Milestown."

"How's he paying you?"

"Very well, and with a bonus if we finish up by the end of the month."

"That's not what I asked. Give me a straight answer."

The man shifted his feet. "A draft on a Fort Benton company, I. G. Baker, Herr Sergeant."

"Quigby's from Fort Benton?"

"I don't know, sir. If you'd like, I'll ask him to go to your Fort and see you."

"Naw. You bohunks or honyockers or whatever, you get outa here and back to your homesteads. Right now. You leave this be. That's an army order. You git! You git or you'll have the army running you out.''

Tollefson looked frightened. He stared nervously at Wiltz, taking in the sergeant's massive, deadly bulk, and then at the two noncoms with him.

"I can't do that. We make a contract and keep it. Contracts, they are made by honor, ja?"

"You heard me.''

"I think maybe I will talk to the commander at the Fort. Let us go, then. I will walk.''

"You ain't talking to the commander. You're just going to pack up and git.''

"Can you do that? I thought in America the government could not . . . This is private land, ja?"

"In Indian country the army does what it has to, Tollefson. You'd better understand that.''

"But if we go we don't get paid! You are taking bread and butter from us, from our children!"

"You heard me, Tollefson.''

The man looked stubborn and angry. He drew himself up. "Then you will have to drive us away. Drive us like cattle! There is no law I know of against building this building for a wage.''

Tollefson's defiant stare astonished Wiltz. He wasn't used to it. Twenty years in the army had taught him to pound defiant men into the earth, like bugs. His temper flared hot, but he held it in. Wade's warning hung in his mind. That and his sergeant major's instinct about the limits of his power. He'd gotten where he was by knowing when not to cross certain lines, when to say no to his instinct to mash noses and bust bones and crack heads.

He smiled suddenly. "Go back to your building, Tollefson.''

The waiting drove Mordecai Sapp mad. The stupid Norwegian perfectionists took forever and would not be hurried. Sometimes they wasted hours undoing a board that didn't fit, or one that had cracked, or one too warped. They seemed to think they were building a guildhall rather than a dive. He visited them every few days, shortly after dark when they were still up and about, and railed at Tollefson. Then, riding back to

Miles and some saloon refreshments, he regretted his anger. The wound had done that to him. He was losing control of himself. That and other things, he thought. He could scarcely call himself the child of two Utopians in Indiana.

In fact he was still discovering the ultimate effect of that bullet through his brain. His leg and arm hadn't improved, and that peeved him. It'd make gambling harder when his fingers scarcely worked. But there'd been other things. Taste. Appetite. He'd lost most of his sense of taste, and could detect little more than salt. Meat and bread had turned to cardboard; it had all become foul mush he had to swallow. He'd almost quit eating and had lost weight rapidly, so fast that his Fort Benton clothing hung loose and baggy. That was reason enough to murder Wiltz. He'd always loved his food: bacon, eggs, rhubarb pie, chocolate cake, coffee, fine Kentucky bourbon, maple syrup. Gone, all gone, transformed to pulp. And more. His left eyelid drooped now, and his throat had gone spastic at times so he couldn't swallow. And more . . . the thing he dreaded the most. He was almost certain he could no longer pleasure a dolly. He hadn't tried it yet, but he knew, he knew. What good was life half-ruined? In his bleaker moments conscience tore at him. Perhaps he'd gotten what he deserved.

Frequently now he paced his room in the Nelson Miles Hotel in a nervous rage, sensing mounting danger each day he lurked there. He didn't emerge at all by daylight, knowing that some in Milestown would recognize him. He grew a beard and it came in streaked with white, but it changed his appearance. So the days were endless and filled with small and large terrors, as pairs of soldiers patrolled the town. So far, only enlisted men. He studied them from his window as he'd once studied rattlesnakes. He scarcely knew what he'd do if Sergeant Wiltz and his bullyboys showed up. He'd railed at Quigby to hurry up. The man had done nothing but snoop and probe around, like some fool coward, instead of getting on with it.

Sometimes, at dusk, he'd hurried out with Popskull into the soft summer nights and limped quietly down to Bug's Saloon, a cottonwood log affair and the lowest of the low-life hangouts in Miles, and there he'd slid into a safe corner seat and drunk large tumblers of redeye and watched the yeggs and footpads and hooligans there while they watched him, pointing at the gold metal that glowed like mad beacons from his skull. Sapp knew what they were thinking. Gold. He watched them with his knowing eye even while they watched the gold covering his brain, and he wished that damned Dr. Toole had hammered silver dollars for his holes instead of eagles. His gold patches glowed like fireballs in Bug's Saloon, while around him men pointed and smirked. Silver would have tarnished to dark brown, like liver spots, and have become almost invisible.

"How's Goldie tonight?" asked the barkeep once, but Sapp silenced him with a murderous glare, and the subject was never mentioned again.

One night two had followed him out, after he'd sated his wild thirst. Followed him, soft in the velvet blackness of an unlit street a block off Main. Followed him, creeping up upon his gold. He didn't hesitate. He slipped his revolver from his coat pocket, swung, and shot, two shattering blasts in the night. One man fell, the other rushed in. A third blast, a flash of light from his muzzle, and the other one sank into the dust. His throat spasmed again. His feet wouldn't work, but he willed himself into a black alley, saw no one, and slipped to his hotel.

The next morning he sent Quigby off to Gatz's store to buy a derby. He refused to go himself. They measured Sapp's head with a string but it still took two tries. The second black derby slid tightly—almost too tightly, making his wounds hurt—over his ivory flesh, tight over his ear, covering both gold patches. From that moment on, Sapp knew, that derby would never come off his head except in bed. He stared at himself in a looking glass, scarcely recognizing the image; the gaunt, lean face, the vanished jowls, the drooping eyelid, the sagging lower lip he discovered and blamed on his wounding, and a body turning thin. The next day he set a seamstress to work refitting his baggy clothing.

"You might as well wander around, Sapp. No one would ever recognize you now," said Quigby.

"Heed your own counsel."

Quigby irked him. The pudgy man had not fulfilled his contract. Not one noncom. And his pleasure palace would open in just a few days.

The soft pink man smiled. "You're a prisoner of your own fears, Sapp. Goodness gracious. You've changed. Lost sixty pounds, I'd say. The beard. Lean face. The derby—not a soul would recognize you except yourself. The Good Book says that the evil flee when no man pursueth, or something to that effect. Very odd, Sapp. You're the victim. The army did you in. And here you are, acting guilty, cowering in this room."

Sapp found himself fascinated and enraged by this audacious observation. A victim, yes. Why had he been acting like a man on the lam?

"Do your job, Quigby, and heed your own counsel. You're much overdue."

"Just thought I'd be helpful, Sapp. You can't be in our profession and hide from your thoughts. My goodness. I've dealt with all this. You must have a certain modern view of the universe or else live in terror. I'm purely a rational modern man without superstition as far as possible, and I fashion myself an instrument of justice because divine justice doesn't exist. I recommend that you deal with your ghosts or get out. Go south."

Quigby had said all this so deferentially, so hesitantly and apologetically, that Sapp scarcely imagined he was being lectured. But somehow Quigby had the upper hand, servant had become master, and that fact vastly irritated Sapp.

"Do your duty or forget your reward!" Sapp snarled.

"Now that will happen any day, Sapp. The new building is bound to be discovered any moment, and when it happens our problems will be solved. Goodness gracious! Wiltz is perfectly predictable. He'll lead the same group of conspirators out there to burn the place and drive off your carpenters. I'll arrange an incident." He smiled, filled with beatific joy. "No more noncoms. And a few immigrants will be hanged. I've never arranged a riot before, but it has endless possibilities, especially when the rioters don't know English."

"I don't want immigrants hanged."

"Scruples, Sapp? Odd, odd how you've changed. Did that bullet drill morals into you? Mercy me! They won't be hanged. They'll merely be defending themselves against criminal arsonists. But I threw that in just to show you how you've changed."

Quigby seemed to be toying with him.

"Now don't overheat, Mordecai. Goodness sakes. My task is to show my employer every contingency, every implication beforehand, so you may proceed with stout felonious heart."

Sapp wasn't mollified. He peered sharply at the chubby, pink man whose manipulative mind pulled and shoved him with such ease.

"I think," said Quigby, glancing out the window, "that we'll be having visitors shortly."

Sapp peered out upon Main Street and froze. A block or so west three blue-bloused riders approached: Sergeant Major Wiltz and Corporals Liggett and Horn.

"They'll probably come here, looking for Quigby. That's the name you gave to the Norwegians, Sapp. Let them find me, not you. The moment's come, Sapp. You can shoot them down on the street, or you can see if they recognize you. I'll wager they won't give you more than a passing glance. Your beard alone will do it."

Quigby peered blandly at Sapp, as if making a humble request, but Sapp took it for a command. He'd come under the spell of some malign and powerful intelligence.

He peered out. Half a block now. Still time to reach the street. He gathered his walking stick and limped out the door, rapping down hotel stairs, wild fear pulsing in him, plummeting through the hotel door moments before the noncoms on three cavalry mounts drew up. He felt their gaze instantly and ignored it, rapping down the boardwalk toward Gatz's store.

Behind him he heard the sudden clop of hooves and a horseman pulled alongside.

"You."

Sapp peered boldly at Wiltz, never breaking stride but ready to draw his revolver and shoot.

"Never mind," said Wiltz. But then the sergeant seemed to have second thoughts. "Your name Quigby?"

"Far from it."

"What's your business?"

"Performing extreme unction upon soldiers."

"Haw!" said Wiltz. "That's rich."

Chapter 14

The three soldiers who bulled their way into his room filled the whole space, making Januarius Quigby twitch. Wiltz grabbed the plump drummer by the shirt, patted him down with massive paws, discovered the small revolver in its underarm holster, and plucked it with a malicious growl. The others, Corporals Horn and Liggett, popped valises, poked through clothing, dumped out the contents of Quigby's sample case.

From a corner Popskull rose up, the ruff of hair around his neck pricking out, and snarled, yellow-eyed. Horn backed off in a hurry.

"Sapp's wolf!" cried Liggett.

Wiltz shoved, and Quigby found himself careening smack into the wall behind him.

"Gentlemen," he gasped. "What brings you—"

"Cut the crap, Quigby. You've been messing around the Fort, peddling your quack ointments. You got a bunch of Norwegians building a dive. You got Sapp's wolf."

"Sapp? Who's that?"

Wiltz laughed.

"It sounds like the juice of a tree," Quigby muttered.

The animal growled, baring vicious canines and driving the corporals away from its corner.

"That's a wolf? Goodness. I wouldn't know a wolf from a German shepherd. The poor starving brute followed me on my rounds, whimpering, hungry. I took pity on the beast, you see. My soul reaches out to unfortunate creatures, human and canine."

131

"Sure, Quigby. You got some connection with Sapp? What're you building out there?"

"I can't imagine who this Sapp is," Quigby said. "Goodness gracious, won't you treat a drummer kindly? Some people are like that. Think all we do is twist arms and cheat. Oh, mercy, what have I done?"

These noncoms alarmed him, slapping him about and not even waiting for explanations. Fear and loathing boiled through him, not only of these brutes but Sapp as well, who'd used his name while dealing with the carpenters. Used his name! Made a spectacle of him, against all the rules of his profession.

"Were you some silent partner of Sapp's, cleaning up on Hogtown and rebuilding now?" Wiltz demanded.

Quigby managed to look bewildered. "Building? I'm not building anything. What is this place, Hogtown? Where is it?"

"Carpenters said you hired 'em."

"I've never hired anyone. I'm a manufacturer's rep. I can show you my travel route, my territory. Always on the move. Mercy, there's been some mistake, gentlemen!"

"Sales rep with a gat in a shoulder holster."

"Mercy! This is wild country! Stagecoach bandits, wild Indians, ruffians. Why, I almost used it on that poor mutt when it threatened me. Before I realized it was begging, of course."

"Carpenters said you hired 'em."

"There's some mistake. A coincidence. Maybe there's another Quigby, or Quinby. I'm Januarius. You ask them if I was the one. Better yet, let's go out there—see if they recognize me!"

"Maybe we will, Quigby."

The bulgy man began to gather courage. "I'm simply here to sell valuable things. Gore and Son Apothecary Goods. Why, I'm pleased that you, Corporal, ordered one of our—"

"Cut it, Quigby."

Januarius Quigby had never been thus addressed in his life. Nor had his portmanteaus been searched and his haberdashery pitched about. Not by private citizens or police. But the army . . . A crescendo of hate erupted through him, causing him to smile humbly.

"Take me to these carpenters. I insist upon it to clear my

good name. If you think ill of my virtue and probity, you'll not purchase my wares, and I'd grieve and count my days here lost. I'll fetch a buggy and a dray from the livery stable and we'll go at once."

He began sorting through his samples, poking them back into his sample case. "I may as well take this and maybe sell a few things to these people," he said shyly. "Mercy heavens."

The noncoms stared skeptically.

"Let's go, then," he said, straightening his attire. He eyed Popskull. "You stay here, little wolfie. Daddy'll feed you when he returns."

"Might as well do it," Wiltz muttered.

"Ah, I'd like my little self-protector back."

"This thing?" Wiltz eyed the small, five-shot, .32-caliber hideout revolver. He grinned broadly. "Yeah, sure. Good for rabbits."

Good for eyeballs, hearts, and testicles, Quigby thought, sliding it back into its familiar and comforting locale. He straightened his cravat and they trooped out the door.

An hour later Quigby, escorted by three riders, wheeled his buggy into the gulch where Hogtown was rising once again, after being careful to ask directions from Wiltz. Tollefson saw them coming and waited, looking testy.

"Who's this?" Wiltz demanded. "He hire you?"

Tollefson glared. "I never see him before. No. The one hired us is big, big. And what is the matter with hiring us? We do a fine job, an honest day's labor from dawn to dusk."

"Tollefson, I'm going to pound you. . . ."

Others of the Norwegian men gathered around, and Tollefson addressed them. They stared at Quigby, shook their heads. "No, no," they said.

"I don't think this Quigby's the one, Sarge," said Liggett. Wiltz glared.

"Tollefson, what was the name of the one that hired you, again?"

"Quigby," he said, "but not this man. Bigger."

"Who are you sharing that hotel room with, Quigby?" Wiltz asked. "That clerk said—"

"Why . . . a reverend. Some offbeat sect. A phrenologist, I believe. You know, they read character from the bumps on your head. Met in the stagecoach and thought to save a bit. . . ."

"What's his name?"

"Why, his last name I don't know. Calls himself the Great Pondoro. I call him Mort. Now as long as I'm here, I'd like to represent my products. Mr. Tollefson, I have a sample here of something you'll find invaluable, a tonic—"

"No money for tonics. We make our own tonics from the herbs," the carpenter said.

"Well, I'll leave a small sample so that you can discover the priceless secret of—"

"Let's get outa here, Sarge," said Horn.

Wiltz nodded. "Quigby, I got my eye on you. If I see you around Keogh I'll pulp you, I'll turn you to wolf dinner. I'll gouge your eyes out and feed them to hens."

"Heh, heh, army humor's new to me," Quigby said.

He watched them ride off and felt his tension leak from him like beer going flat. Around him, carpenters shuffled off and the sounds of hammering and sawing resumed. He turned the dray back toward Miles, driving absently, his mind upon larger things.

Every rule violated. He'd become the focus of attention, someone they'd remember. Deep obscurity, invisibility, gone. His name known. That incredible fool Sapp had used it wantonly, without the slightest consideration. . . . He'd finally been forced to lie, to invent, to create an identity for Sapp, which could get them into instant trouble. Even now, the non-coms might be riding to Miles rather than the Fort, to look for the Great Pondoro and find—Mordecai Sapp. The only comfort was that so far he'd only reconnoitered. He had yet to begin operations, get down to business.

Suddenly grateful for his caution, he knew perfectly what he must do: abandon this one, get out, vanish. Money lost, to be sure, but safety had always been his first priority. Sapp had proved to be a blunderer and fool. No one to ally himself to, for certain. Maybe he'd better take measures against Sapp himself, just to keep mouths closed. The thought preoccupied him as he drove along the rutted road and into Milestown late in the afternoon.

He found Mordecai Sapp in the room, feeding bones to Popskull.

"Listen well, brother Sapp. We're out of danger, but not entirely." He described his roughing up by Wiltz, the trip to Hogtown, and Sapp's new identity.

"The Great Pondoro," Sapp said, testing the name succulently. "I'll read your noodle, Januarius. That bump over your ear says you've a criminal mind."

"There's more, Sapp. This episode puts me in danger. Violates all my rules. I always work invisibly. I'm out. Leaving on the next stage south."

"You can't. We've a contract. I've paid—"

"You paid half, yes. And violated the contract. You used my name to hire those carpenters. I'm a salesman. Only a salesman."

Quigby wished he'd kept silent and simply pulled out without warning. But that had risks, too.

"I want my money back," Sapp snarled.

"I've performed services. Hired your dollies, run your errands, run risks. We're even, Sapp. As long as you failed to keep confidences."

The master of Hogtown glowered at him silently, murder in his eye, his derby askew. Januarius organized his valises, filled his portmanteau with clothing, and added a hotel towel.

Mordecai Sapp stood, leaning heavily on his walking stick. "Quigby, let's part friendly," he said gently.

Januarius turned at the door, pausing. Sapp smiled, lumbered up. The ebony walking stick swept upward, thrust at Quigby's soft middle, and astonishment exploded in Quigby's brain as spring-loaded steel seared deep into his belly.

"Go, Popskull!" Sapp yelled in a falsetto voice.

The wolf catapulted from the carpet, a flying monster, and Quigby felt canines piercing through the thin cartilage of his throat and hot blood gushing down into his lungs as he toppled to the floor. He saw yellow eyes and heard an insane snarling. He felt teeth tearing his face apart, canines piercing his cheeks, and then he felt nothing.

*   *   *

Caution crept into Sergeant Major Wiltz like a shot of redeye. He rode quietly back to Fort Keogh, dismissed the corporals, and reported to Colonel Wade that indeed a structure of some sort was rising at Hogtown; that its purpose and ownership remained a mystery; and that no untoward incidents had occurred. The CO looked testy, so Wiltz beat a retreat to his palacial quarters, carved from three rooms in the noncom barracks, thanks to under-strength garrisoning.

He undid his boots, rubbed his bunions, examined the almost-healed bullet crease in his armpit, and scratched his privates, still remembering the white pain that had bolted through him from Toole's kick. He would never forget that kick from that rinkydink sheriff. Then, in August twilight, he uncorked a quart of ale he'd paused to buy in Miles, settled into a rocker he'd imported from Missouri, and hunkered down to think.

Caution. He hated the feeling but respected it. Caution had bailed him out over and over. No one ever made sergeant major, or stayed there, without it. Caution reminded him that men set in authority over him could ruin him fast. The army did that—ruined men, chopped them up and spit them out and ground the pieces in dirt. Not just sergeants, either. Everyone on the ladder, right up to generals. The army could geld him so fast he'd scarcely know what happened. Make him a private, strip him of pay, pop him into a guardhouse, write up a record that'd haunt him in outside life. No . . . he mustn't despise caution when it pounced on him, as it did now.

He guzzled a pint, feeling the foam fizz in his throat, and then belched loudly. Caution. Sense enough to leave those Norwegian carpenters alone, for one. Let them build the thing. He could always torch it later, after they'd gone back to homesteading and weren't witnesses. Wade would've landed on him if he'd driven them off—an incident, civilians roaring and howling, Wiltz's tender old hemorrhoids in bleedin' trouble.

Caution. Take Horn, now. The man had turned resentful, sullen all day, sore about doing any more dirty errands. Wiltz had noticed it, sensed the danger in it. Horn knew. Horn could talk. Horn was a witness. Horn could spill his guts to Toole or Wade. A man about to be ticketed out saw things differently, old loyalties gone. He'd have to watch Horn. Maybe get him out faster—yes, that was it. He'd talk Wade into mustering out Horn at once, tomorrow, save payroll, all the rest. The sooner he got Horn out of Keogh, the safer his secrets would be. He'd lay it on the colonel first thing in the morning.

Toole. He'd like to kill that skinny sheriff, but it'd be trouble. Killing a doctor. Maybe just boot him in the lights. The sheriff kept probing, messing around, asking too many questions. Not getting much, not enough to put a case together anyway. . . . Maybe lifting them spent bullets and burnt revolver wasn't so smart. Tampering with evidence. The stuff he'd lifted from Toole's office lay before him, incriminating him, right on the table. Caution. Give it to Wade; make it look like he'd picked up the stuff for official purposes, for the inquiry. . . .

Toole he'd watch. The sheriff had hit dead ends, and he'd give up soon. Unless he really did have a witness. Unlikely. And if he had a witness, he'd be parading the man— or was it a man?—in Wade's office. Sapp. Vernon Wiltz snorted. Sapp had been eaten by fish. He'd shot Sapp himself, blew the man's brains out, held a lantern over the corpse, saw the gray brains all over the logs. Not Sapp. Some dolly? He stirred restlessly, sucked another long draught of ale, and belched comfortably. He could belch the length of three heartbeats, and in several tones. He was an expert with gasses and figured he could replace any bugler in Keogh.

Who the hell owned the new Hogtown? Not Sapp. Probably not that butterball pink drummer. Well, waiting would tell him. Let it open. Let it begin. Maybe it'd be just what Tollefson said, a saloon and dance hall. Hurdy-gurdy. Dime a dance. Genteel; milk soldiers slow and soft instead of fast and hard. That'd be better than the Hogtown anyway. Enlisted men wouldn't lift army property for a spin around a dance floor. Caution. Wait and see. The new dump might even be a classy place to go. He wondered irritably why he'd been hell-bent to torch it. On the other hand, hurdy-gurdies could be rough. Knockout drops, bar girls. . . . He'd quietly post a few noncoms at the new dump, get a sense of the joint. Caution. . . .

He drained the last of the ale, peeved that payday lay ten days ahead and sergeants major earned about enough for a week of ale and three weeks of dry spit. He'd given his life to the goddamn army, and the army never returned the favor.

He heard the melody, and stood. Mess, time for mess. Time for caution.

Next morning he waited until Wade had had his third mug of black coffee. The colonel could not be approached before that. Wiltz had gotten that from various adjutants and sergeants. They all kept a book on each officer. Three Mugs Wade, they called the CO.

"Got some things for you, sah," he said, noting that a half-inch of black java remained in the vitreous white mug. Wade looked testy.

"Get on with it. I don't have all day."

"These here, sah, are evidence gathered at Hogtown by Sheriff Toole."

He laid the spent bullets and the scorched revolver on Wade's desk.

"I thought, sah, since he's incapac— since he's hurt, that I'd help matters along. For the inquiry, sah. Picked them up over at the doctor's house a while back and forgot to give them to you. Toole'll be grateful, I'm sure. No doubt meanin' to bring these items to you before he got hurt."

"That was dumb, Wiltz. Picking up evidence. Your brains have been in your little toe for a month now. I'll talk to Toole about it. I can confiscate it if I want, but I want to know what this stuff means."

"Very good, sah. I was thinkin' of the army; just wasn't too smart about it."

Wade stared, incredulous. "Are you well, Wiltz?"

"Couldn't be better, sah. Now another matter here. These papers will discharge Corporal Horn. He's not getting any better; that arm's gone. His morale's down. No sense his waiting around. I thought to save the post a bit; send him off."

"Aren't you full of charity. It's who-you-know in the army, eh, Sergeant? Horn been hounding you for an early out, I suppose. Well, who've you got replacing him in Company E?"

"LeMat, sah."

Wade frowned. "Not as good as Horn. That Horn was a Reb

sergeant, know that? A lot of experience under fire. Hard to replace experience like that.''

''Right, sah. That's why I'm doing a small favor.''

''Very well. This frees him. Muster him out properly and make damn sure no army property walks off.''

''I'll do it, sah. Wonder how he'll like the outside?''

Wade frowned. ''That's a dumb thing to ask about a man with a bad arm and no profession.''

Wiltz laughed respectfully.

The colonel signed the form and thrust it at Wiltz. ''Tell him to stop by and shake hands. Ah, which arm, Wiltz?''

''Let you guess, Colonel.''

He found Horn in the noncom barracks, trying to wrestle a shirt on one-handed. The corporal's injury had made life's small tasks annoying, and he cursed softly.

''What you need is a dolly, Horn. Button and unbutton. They're good at that.''

''Shut up, Wiltz. Ah got to live with this and you make fun of it. Ah got this on that goddamn private raid of yours rather than duty or war, and Ah'm ready to—''

''Here's your papers. Mustering out today.''

''Today? What the hell? Ah got over a week left before Hoffmeister certifies—''

''All took care of. You're out. Don't you walk off with nothing army, either, or I'll come after you, bust you up. Colonel wants you should shake hands. Where you going? Texas?''

Horn stared at his pay envelope, his discharge, and then at Wiltz.

''I figured you're a bit antsy around here. I cut a little piece of pie for you. Look in here. Ticket on the noon Kinnear stage to Cheyenne and the railroad.''

Horn looked sour. ''You're in some almighty rush to get rid of a ole friend. Ah hardly got time to tell all good-bye.''

''Easier that way, pal.''

''Ah was going to have a party, goddamn you.''

Wiltz shrugged and grinned. Horn would be off in hours, and the weak link would vanish.

Chapter 15

Nothing in his tawdry life astonished Mordecai Sapp more than what he'd just done. It'd simply happened, without thought. Murder had boiled through his brain, a sudden red command, and murder he'd done. He knew, suddenly, that the brain injury had caused it. The bullet had changed him, subjected him to sudden gusts of rage, fried away restraint, turned him into an impulsive butcher.

He'd killed before, or rather he'd hired it done. He'd taken abuse at Hogtown from soldiers, from brutal buffalo-runners aiming to pulverize him, from crooks and sharps, some of them wearing army blues. He'd taken it, weighed odds and chances, and then nodded to Herold, his pox-faced powder-monkey to do it. All coldly considered. Never impulsive, never an orgasmic convulsion of will, such as this.

But there before the door lay Quigby, spread like a Maltese cross, quiet as granite. One moment sentient, now cooling meat. Blood coagulated and browned on the floor, not from his belly wound but near the neck, where Popskull's powerful jaws had torn the throat apart and set carotids pumping blood out upon worn planking. Quigby still looked surprised, astounded by the impossible, the thing beyond his calculation. The scheming little devil had failed to scheme enough.

Twilight. Supper hour passed. Miles was winding up for its nightly roister. Mordecai settled himself on the striped blue bed ticking, feeling the corn husk stuffing whisper under him. He had time but no plan. This wouldn't be discovered until morning—hours away. He could flee, but why? The sheriff lay

140

abed at Keogh; no one else cared much. Not a soul knew Quigby; not a soul grieved him. His departure would no more be remarked than his arrival. If he disappeared, if a drummer left town, who'd know or care?

The river. The restless Yellowstone, just a few city blocks north of here. At Hogtown, the river had taken care of everything. The poxy kid had dragged the stiffs down to the river and splashed them in, farewell and goodbye. A little risky—the stiffs could be snagged anywhere along the restless shores. The river, then. If he could find a way, given his limp and weak arm. Hire a dray. Wait for the small hours of the morning when the night lay deep and solemn over Miles. Hoist him out the window, let him fall to the rutted street. Lift him into the wagon, and drive down to the river. Sample cases too, loaded with rock. Clothing likewise.

Quigby, he raged, what did you do that for? Welshing on an agreement. Cheating me. Not that you were much of an assassin, Quigby, sulking about, too timid to do your duty. Good riddance, Quigby; I can hire a dozen toughs from the saloons, from Bug's alone, who'd enjoy perforating a few noncoms.

Mordecai stared at the fat corpse, feeling its reprimand. Quigby's smudgy brown eyes remained open, staring at him, rebuking him. Annoyed, Mordecai turned away. The wait would be a long one. And he had to rent a dray for overnight, return it in the morning, a weak link, something a hostler would remember, since Sapp had rented only for evenings before. Maybe he could simply drag Quigby down to the river, even with one good arm and leg.

Popskull licked his red-stained chops. Sapp fed him another beef bone from the butcher shop.

He often rented a dray this time of evening to drive out to the new dive. Returned it in the middle of the evening and walked on over to Bug's for his nightly redeye. Perhaps . . .

A half hour later Sapp reined up before the hotel in a spring wagon drawn by an old mare. Dark had descended, and only amber lantern light from the hotel desk illuminated the murky street. He saw no one. At the other end of Miles the saloon patrons were hunkering down to serious swilling, but here the night swallowed Main Street.

Sweating, he clambered up the stairs and then slid open the sash window of his room. It clattered down, refusing to stay put. He propped it up with a coat hanger. Then he dumped Quigby's clothing out, regretting that he couldn't sell it. He limped down the wooden stairs with Quigby's sample cases and portmanteau, and dropped these in the wagon. No witnesses so far. Rutherford, the hotel clerk, had vanished to his quarters as usual, and could be summoned only with the loud clamor of a bell.

Panting, Sapp pushed the luggage to the front of the wagon box. Then he idled impatiently as a hotel patron, an elderly man, shuffled out the front door and vanished down the street. Sapp watched him go, watched his dim figure vanish into an eatery a block away. He lumbered up the stairs again, feeling his heart protest. He snuffed the lantern in his room and peered out the open window. Nothing. A great peace in this corner of Milestown. He lifted Quigby's arm, astonished by its coldness. How could short Quigby weigh so much? Sapp puffed and dragged Quigby to the window and hoisted the legs upward, while Popskull watched intently, his yellow eyes picking up distant rays of light.

Gasping, Sapp wrestled Quigby upward, fighting the supple deadweight, until at last he'd perched the tubby assassin on the windowsill. He peered sharply into the night, each way, up and down. He listened for noises below. Nothing. The risky part now. He shoved. The body somersaulted through space and smacked the clay below, rolling over. Sapp tossed the bed blanket after, for a cover, and lumbered downstairs, thumping along as fast as he could make his slow leg work.

Outside, movement a half block away. Someone coming. Wildly Sapp peered around. He could drag Quigby into a dark alley and wait it out. No, he thought, load and leave. The dray mare shifted and cocked a rear leg. A fresh pile lay at her feet. Winded, Sapp dragged the drummer to the wagon and wrestled him upward, finding strength through sheer will. The dumpy drummer rolled in a heap. Sapp snatched the blanket and covered the corpse, and turned wildly to observe the stroller's progress.

A stranger ambled close, features unfathomable in the blackness. Sapp sagged against the wagon, his good hand gripping his revolver in its underarm niche. Popskull eyed Sapp quizzically, ready to jump.

"Nice night," said the man, his gaze casually taking in the wagon with its blanketed load.

"Cool enough to travel," Sapp muttered.

The man wandered by.

Sapp scrambled to the wagon seat, set the dray in motion, and Popskull jumped aboard. Sapp headed eastward, away from the west-end saloons, from Keogh, from Hogtown. And downriver. Yes, especially downriver. He drove softly into the night, feeling his body relax, his pulse return to normal, picking his way by starlight because the moon hadn't yet risen. The soft, jolting rhythm of the wagon, the crunch of iron tires, the thump of hooves, all settled his tumults.

Behind him, Quigby's corpse rolled under the blanket. A breeze curled the blanket off, exposing Quigby's bobbing head and gory throat, bringing bile up in Sapp. Quigby had been soft in life and stayed pillowy in death. Suddenly Sapp brimmed with red rage. He loathed the drummer who'd done this to him, forced him to kill, to sweat, to peer at dark corners with wild terror, to exert himself beyond his strength. Rage. He snarled, yanked the mare to a halt, grabbed the whip from its socket and jumped down. Flailed Quigby with the whip, lashing down and down over the rubbery corpse, biting at flesh with the tassel, flailing until his good arm weakened and ached. From the front wagon seat, Popskull watched amiably. The mare, knowing the shrill of a whip, lurched forward. Sapp stared, sweat beading on his brow, and bolted after the wagon, catching the mare only because she grew lazy a hundred yards distant. Sapp clambered up, trembling, and wiped sweat away from his eyes, finished with his vespers.

An hour and perhaps four miles later, Sapp discerned a place where the trace veered close to the river. Good enough, he thought, carefully steering the mare out upon brown grasses. She stopped suddenly and would go no further. Sapp found himself at a low cliff sloping down to a river bottom filled with brush, and twenty yards beyond, the black river, pricked by stars on the wavering water.

Good enough. More work. Trembling with exhaustion now, Sapp tumbled Quigby off, rolled him over the lip, dragged him through brush, and kicked him off the bank, enjoying a satisfying splash. The dark thing bobbed and twisted away, rotating once. Good-bye, Quigby, he thought gleefully. He spat into the water, a parting shot. He rested, then found loose sandstone with which to sink the portmanteau and sample cases and pitched them wearily with his weakening good arm. They sank into the oily waters, releasing bubbles that caught in the starlight. He lacked strength to weight down the clothes, tie them to rocks, so he simply ditched them in the dense brush. Some redskins would show up wearing the stuff some day.

Relieved, he floundered his way up the steep slope and collapsed in the wagon seat. Popskull leaped up beside him, dragging something. Something of Quigby's.

"No, Popskull," he muttered. He tugged, but Popskull snarled. Clothing of some sort. He tugged again, and Popskull let it go, snapping wildly, berserk. Sapp tumbled back, the clothing in hand, but he dropped it, tossed it back to the violent beast, who snapped it up in midair.

Let the damned wolf chew, Sapp thought. For a moment the carmine rage exploded through him, and he reached for his revolver. Kill the wolf! Then, shaking, he slumped into his wagon seat, and drove back. There'd be a few things still to do; the blood on the floor, check everything, check his own clothing. Do it all, fast, and be done.

He felt no relief. Quigby floated miles away, fish food, but still seemed to fill the wagonbed.

Corporal Horn gone. Discharged that morning.

"I don't understand it," muttered Dr. Hoffmeister. "In a few days I am to test him, certify he's got no use of that arm for the records. This army is mad with records. But no, the corporal is on the stagecoach now and no one has come to consult me. A medical discharge? Ach!"

Santiago's mind raced. Horn gone, and along with Horn, any hope of a confession. Wiltz's work obviously. The sergeant major was no dummy, and danced ahead of Santiago one way or another. The sheriff settled back on his cot, testy and bitter, feeling trapped by his wounds, the hospital, the post. He had to get out.

As soon as Hoffmeister wandered out of the room he flipped his sheet back, swung his legs to the floor, and sat up. An amazing pain lanced through his chest, hot and evil, paralyzing the motoring of his lungs. Then dizziness, whirling and bobbing, until he careened back into bed again, stunned by his weakness.

He sank into the bedclothes smouldering with rage and frustration, seeing his investigation slide through his fingers while he lay helpless. He lay in the clammy sheets sullenly, wanting to do something, anything, building up a fine Irish temper.

That's when Colonel Orville Prescott Wade penetrated his reveries. Santiago peered up and saw the CO standing before him, puffy and dour.

"Get out of my room!" Santiago roared, wincing at the hurt of his roaring.

Nonplussed, the CO stared. "This happens to be my command, Toole."

"And I happen to be a civilian, a sheriff and a doctor. Now get the hell out or I'll throw you out."

Wade blinked. He reddened. Then he deflated slowly like a tired bellows. "I'm going to chat with you, Toole. We're going to discuss evidence. The progress of my inquiry. And other matters."

"Other matters like Horn. You shipped out one of my suspects. More than suspect. He murdered a civilian in my district and never mind that the civilian needed murdering. That civilian shot him in the arm and you know it. You don't believe that gun-cleaning story any more than I do, experienced soldier like Horn." Santiago had been shouting, but now he quieted down. "Wade, you shipped him out an inch ahead of a warrant. You're frustrating justice and by God I'll serve you and throw you in my slammer when it's built if you don't get him back here and—"

"Toole, you're cracked."

"You wait and see."

"It was Wiltz. The sergeant major arranged it for morale reasons. I scarcely had anything to do with it."

"Wiltz. Of course. He organized that little massacre. Horn was the weak link, the one who might talk. Well, Wade, I'll hang Wiltz."

The thought of Vernon Wiltz dangling from a noose so plainly astonished Colonel Wade that he gaped at Santiago. Then he frowned, reinflated himself, thrust out his chin, waggled his waxed mustache tips, and glared. "May I remind you," he said acidly, "that you're being held here by the United States Army pending an inquiry."

"You just try holding a civilian and a sheriff! I've got a letter off to the governor. Wait until that lion roars, Wade. Just try holding me!"

Toole ran out of breath. His chest radiated menacing pain, and he suddenly wanted an anodyne.

"The governor?"

"The governor. It describes my case and my evidence—which Wiltz tampered with—stole, actually. And the unwillingness of officers here to act or cooperate. Cover-up, Wade. You're covering up a massacre."

The colonel's eyes bagged, and he blinked. "That's what I came about. Sergeant Major Wiltz turned over the bullets and the revolver he confiscated. Of course I plan to introduce the materials in our own inquiry."

"Oh he did, did he? Got a little nervous, did he? Wanted to make it look nice and proper, did he? When was this?"

"This morning."

"What's it been, Wade? Almost a month since his goons beat me and he stole evidence right out of my office? Why didn't he turn it over to you right away?"

Toole glared, and Wade couldn't meet the glare.

"I'll note the delay in my next report!" Toole yelled.

A tic developed in Wade's right cheek. "You gain nothing by shouting at me, Toole."

"All right, I'll talk softly. First to General Sherman, then to General Sheridan, and then to Colonel Miles. About you."

"Generals of the army and commanders of the departments don't tend to give weight to the word of rural sheriffs, Toole. Before all this unpleasant shouting began, I came to inform you that our inquiry begins September 1. If we find cause to do so, we'll bind you over to a federal marshal on federal charges of aiding and abetting theft of government property. You'll be taken east for trial.''

"On what evidence?"

"Testimony of several noncoms that you resisted their dragnet in Milestown.''

Toole sagged back in his pillow. "If the noncoms live that long," he said. "They're marked men.''

"I don't follow you.''

"Sapp.''

"Toole, that concussion's unbalanced you. Sapp vanished.''

"I told you weeks ago. You chose not to believe it. Well, you tell Wiltz's little cabal—the ones who pounded on me and put me in here—to stay alert. Sapp's going to get even.''

"Sapp's ghost, eh? Or whoever's rebuilding Hogtown.''

The news didn't surprise Santiago. "Hogtown's being rebuilt and you still don't believe me?''

"Wiltz investigated yesterday. New owner apparently. Much fancier place, I gather. My staff's looking into it. Sergeant Major Wiltz assured me weeks ago everyone in the old Hogtown had vanished in the fire or after it, and that settles the matter.''

Toole said nothing. He was done talking, tired beyond description.

Colonel Wade stared, wheeled, and walked out.

Santiago closed his eyes. Everything in his body ached, and yet he'd discovered a vitality in himself he hadn't felt since he'd regained consciousness. He'd recover fast now. But Holy Mary, what a little rage had done to him. He braced himself on an elbow and hunted for the blue bottle in his medical valise, pawing past sawbones tools, forceps, spatulum, stethoscope, syringe. He needed the anodyne this one more time. At last, the rectangular blue laudanum bottle. Opium in a tincture of alcohol. Normal dose, five to fifteen drops. Faster than paregoric, the camphorated tincture. He lifted it to his lips with his good arm and swallowed, hoping he'd stayed under fifty drops.

He floated loose of his body, leaving pain down on the cot. Pain lived down below but never up here. His mind sharpened, keen to bring justice to Fort Keogh. He could do so little down there in his cot, waiting for bones to mend and flesh to heal. Corporal Horn gone, slipping through his fingers. And the others so close-mouthed and loyal to each other that he could never crack their cabal. But Sapp! Ah, Sapp! The victim in all of this. Hogtown Sapp, despicable slaver and murderer. What would Sapp do now? Rebuild, yes. Hire new women and saloon men. And then what? Why, hold a party for Fort Keogh. . . .

And what would the noncoms do, discovering Sapp alive and rebuilding? Burn him out and kill him for good. And what would Sapp do, knowing the noncoms would kill him on sight? Why, kill them first! Ah, this laudanum. What clarity! How his mind sailed keenly through the cerulean heaven!

Find Sapp. Bring him down there to his cot for a candid talk, a few questions. Warn him: If he murders noncoms, he'll hang. Ah yes, a hemp noose for Sapp. Extra heavy, with an oversized crossbeam and a sturdy trap, and a large black hood. He'd remind the executioner: everything heavy duty for Sapp and Vernon Wiltz. Heavy-duty rope. Did sheriffs do it here in America? Spring the trap? A fine dilemma for a doctor bound by oath.

And how would a bed-ridden sheriff, trapped in Keogh, reach Mordecai Sapp? Mimi. Mimi knew Sapp lived. She'd seen Sapp. She could find Sapp. Bring Sapp in the middle of the night. Maybe Sapp would tell his story at last, tell Sheriff Toole what had happened at Hogtown, and who, who, who.

Satisfied, and free of pain at last, Santiago Toole navigated back down into his hospital cot and pulled the sheet over him. When Mimi came, he'd set her to tracking Sapp. He'd never seen her so fierce and eager to help.

Chapter 16

Scot-free. No one in Milestown remarked the departure of a drummer named Januarius Quigby. Drummers came and went. Mordecai exulted in his good fortune. He'd scrubbed up the blood on the plank floor, checked the wagon before returning it, gone over the hotel room once again for anything.

Still, there were tricky complications. The room had been rented in Quigby's name. The dollies arriving next week had dealt with Quigby and would be looking for him. Sapp didn't even have a list of their names. He'd have to meet each eastbound stage arriving after the first of September and ask each arriving woman if she was looking for Quigby. Some dollies made their profession obvious when traveling, but others didn't.

He stopped at the hotel desk and told the clerk Quigby had left. He re-registered as Ivan Romanov, and confided that he was a phrenologist and seer. That night he loitered long at Bug's, studying the habitués there while nursing redeye. He didn't want to drink very much; he had business to do. Popskull coiled up at his feet under the table, a comfortable ace in any hole. Sapp thought Bug's would make an excellent employment office. The new Hogtown would open in a week or so and he needed two bartenders, an enforcer, and perhaps a roustabout kid or old drunk who'd swamp out the place for a little booze.

One man in particular intrigued him: a medium-height, skeletal albino who seemed to have no other name than Cottonmouth. He advertised his profession with twin mismatched revolvers tied low on his thighs, one weapon ivory-gripped and the other with grips of checkered walnut.

149

Sapp bought the man a drink.

"Name's Romanov," he said. "And I'm hiring."

"You some kind of Russian?"

"My late father, yes. High in the Imperial Court. But my mother's English and I was raised by her here in the states."

"What are you hiring for?"

"I own the new saloon opening next week up above the Fort. I'm looking for someone to keep order. Someone intelligent and cautious and . . . willing to do whatever's necessary at a nod from me. You'll be dealing mostly with soldiers. Soon, though, big dumb gandy dancers when the railroad comes through. You'd keep the dollies in line but also protect them, eh? You'd have privileges, of course. Any time. You'd be my manager. Make sure the saloon men aren't cheating, and if they are, perform your own executive acts. A hundred a month but also large bonuses for work well done."

The man eyed him coldly from flat white eyes as albino as his flesh and hair. "Five hundred a month," he mumbled.

Sapp sighed. "That's more than I expect to take in a month. Soldiers aren't paid much."

"Sorry," mumbled the albino. "If you want Cottonmouth, you pay Cottonmouth prices."

"Two hundred?"

The man shook his skeletal head.

"Next year, when the tracklayers come, I could do it."

Cottonmouth smiled and tossed back his redeye.

Mordecai actually felt relieved. He wasn't at all sure he wanted Cottonmouth around the place. He might prove unmanageable. Worse, he might drive off customers. The poxy kid had been perfect: dumb, tractable, vicious, willing to do anything. And he cost fifty and found.

"I can see you're a man who doesn't like steady employment."

Cottonmouth shrugged, and signaled Bug for another jolt.

"Perhaps you're more interested in a few small tasks."

Cottonmouth's opaque gaze lifted alertly to Mordecai's.

"Some soldiers. Two sergeants, three corporals."

"What precisely do you have in mind?"

Sapp sighed. He wished these things could go unsaid. "Whatever you choose to do."

"You haven't answered me," Cottonmouth mumbled. "Put it in words and tell me why. I never start any task until I know everything—everything. It saves embarrassments."

"The five soldiers I've mentioned burnt the previous place. Hogtown. Killed the dollies, the previous owner, Sapp, and the saloon men."

"Why?"

"Hogtown was too successful."

"Take off that derby, Goldie. Let me see."

Mordecai froze, then sighed.

"Don't ever lie to me, Sapp. It puts us on a bad footing. Five hundred apiece."

"I can't possibly—"

"You'll earn it in a week when the railroad comes. That's my price. In advance. I take risks; you don't."

"Not all in advance. I've no guarantee. . . ."

"In advance. Gold. Collecting afterward is messy."

A lot of money. Cottonmouth could take it and run. "I tell you what. Half now in gold if there's that much in Milestown, which I doubt. And a credit letter on a Fort Benton account."

"Which you can conveniently cancel before I get to it."

"Fair's fair. You can run with my gold."

Cottonmouth smiled suddenly, revealing a devastated mouth.

"What happened to your teeth?" Mordecai blurted.

"Eighteen sixty-four. One of Beauregard's sergeants slammed them into my throat. Let's try two. A contract for two. Then we'll see about the others. Alarm spreads. They become more difficult, you know."

"You're expensive. I could do it myself."

"With a palsied arm and leg, Sapp? Do you want your new dive to open or not? I'm through dealing."

Mordecai peered around nervously. He didn't want his name bandied about so loudly.

Cottonmouth grinned. "Romanov," he said softly.

"Five hundred for Sergeant Major Wiltz—the ringleader. Three hundred for the rest."

Cottonmouth smiled blandly.

"All right then. You're breaking me but I'll get it back. You're looking for Wiltz, Sergeant Chester Buford, Corporals Max Liggett, André Polanc, and Len LeMat. Polanc and Liggett live on Suds Row. The others in the noncom barracks. There was another they discharged, Cletus Horn. He's left."

"Where?"

"I don't know. By luck, I saw him board the stage a few days ago in civilian duds. One thing, Cottonmouth. You've got less than a week."

"It takes seconds."

"If you'll take greenbacks, we can complete this now."

Cottonmouth stared, and nodded. Mordecai slipped his good hand into his suitcoat, to a special pocket over the kidney, and extracted bills, counting them clumsily in the dull light while Cottonmouth gazed. Mordecai hated it, dishing out money he'd won hard from low-paid soldiers. Most of it from selling off the Fort's goods.

Cottonmouth nodded, smiled, and slipped the green wad into his black britches. "It never takes long," he said.

"If you get Wiltz first, I'll give you a bonus."

Cottonmouth nodded and wandered off toward the batwing door and into the night.

Sapp sucked at his redeye, feeling a thousand dollars lighter and not a guarantee in the world he'd get his money's worth. Wiltz. He'd dreamed of saving Wiltz for himself. He'd planned it that Quigby would get the others, one by one, leaving Wiltz to the last, feeling the noose tighten around him. But he'd discarded that fantasy. Get Wiltz first. Get the most dangerous one first. Get the one most likely to organize another raid on the new Hogtown.

The next evening he rented a trap and drove out to Hogtown in twilight, passing a mob of laughing, excited soldiers walking into Miles. Payday, he realized. They'd blow their entire thirteen dollars in a few hours. It annoyed him that he'd miss this payday. None of them gave him a second glance. The beard and black bowler, the gaunt face added up to a stranger. When he rounded the shoulder and drove toward the new building, what he saw astonished him. Lantern light shone from within, and he heard carpentering even at that late hour.

He found Tollefson waiting for him, smiling.

"Tonight we finish, ja? I'm glad you came; I don't know how to find you. Bonuses, ja? We are early. Come see. It is done to perfection. We build well, to last for a long time."

Mordecai limped up broad porch stairs and into a lamplit saloon, with a splendid bar along the left side and the imported backbar behind it, mirror reflecting the lamps. Everything shone white. White roof beams above, supporting roof planking. A six-lantern chandelier. Creamy walls with built-in benches. Ivory plank floor, smooth for dancing. A dark hallway to the rear. Clean white cubicles with simple wooden bedsteads awaiting a pad or tick. Amazing. The whole thing there before his eyes, days early, attractive, clean. He limped out the back door, feeling rising excitement. There, beyond, lay his own private quarters, away from noise and prying eyes. A three-room cottage: parlor, bedroom, and a kitchen with black and nickel-plate Monarch range and blue chimney pipe all installed, and a zinc sink. Real glass windows in place, reflecting lantern light back at him. Amazing.

Suddenly it had all become real. He had only to ship the furnishings out from the warehouse—the green baize tables, chairs, the bar glasses, the barrels of booze, the new faro layout—ship it out. A little furniture for himself—he'd forgotten that—and he'd be ready. Except for the hiring.

"You like it, ja? You'll rent rooms, too, ja?"

Pleased, he handed letters of credit to Tollefson without a quibble. He'd planned to gyp a little, but the Norwegians had done so well he scarcely thought about it. Tollefson studied the letters drawn on his I. G. Baker account.

"Uffdah! I don't see the bonus, Herr Quigby."

"Oh, the bonus." Sapp had forgotten that. So much of his wealth gone. It gave him dyspepsia. "I'll have to draw it in the morning and send it out. You're going back to your places tonight?"

Tollefson looked worried. "In the morning. Tonight we do the last touches."

"I'll get it to you then," Sapp said shortly.

Tollefson eyed him sharply, but nodded.

Sapp drove back slowly, his mind tumbling with last-minute plans. Ship over the supplies. Hire barmen. Protect the place at once—maybe Cottonmouth'd do that—grand opening. Announce it. Free drinks at first, opening night. Blast, he'd miss payday by a few days. Maybe hire a sporting man to run the gaming tables. Bedclothes. Get blankets from Gatz mercantile. . . .

When he pulled into the livery barn, the hostler, old Blue, seemed agitated.

"You hear it?" he cried. "Couple soldiers shot right on the road betwixt hyar and the Fort. Robbery, they figure, with pockets emptied like that. Yas, shot cold daid. They figger robbery because them sergeants get more pay than the enlisted. Yas, Buford with a hole in his forehead and another right through the left chest. Even stole the buttons offen his britches. And the other, LeMat, same story, robbed and slaughtered."

"That's terrible," said Sapp.

Walking helped. Santiago paced his room and then the corridor, hour after hour. He exercised his arm now that the cast had been cut off, worked his fingers. He unwrapped the heavy bandaging Hoffmeister had wrapped around his chest, and made his lungs work. He pestered the orderlies for fruits and vegetables until they came to fear his rages. He'd increased his time on his feet from two or three minutes to half an hour now, and his time sitting up and out of the cot to most of the day. He'd quit the anodynes, seductive as they were, and preferred instead the dull pain of hard-used muscles and healing flesh.

And he had only one thought in his head: getting out. He'd get out whether or not Wade approved. And there was an odd thing. The forthcoming inquiry had been dropped. Not that Wade had said anything. Or shown him any letter or telegraph from territorial officials or army commanders. In fact, Wade hadn't shown up since Santiago gave him that tongue-lashing, and neither had Wiltz poked his head in. Toole was spoiling to tangle with Wiltz now. Ready to act after weeks helpless on his back, and another week sitting up and staggering around. And still another one pacing crazily, making his body work.

"I think I finally found him," Mimi said, pacing his room

beside him. "It's hard to tell. Do bullets in the head change a person's looks?"

"I suppose it could."

"*Sacre bleu!* I think he's the same one. But he's so different! He's at the Nelson Miles Hotel. He's big but gaunt, not fat. He wears a black derby all the time, inside and out. And a beard with gray streaks. He's well dressed. He looks . . . well, wild-eyed."

"Sapp had a wolf."

"Yes! This one has a big dog that walks behind him. He's registered as Ivan Romanov."

Santiago laughed. "The royal family!"

"I've watched him. He rents a trap evenings. Sometimes he goes over to saloon row."

"Mimi, you didn't walk there at night . . . ?"

"I did. You wanted me to."

"Mimi! I want to get out of here. Right now!"

"Santo, you're not well enough. Dr. Hoffmeister hasn't said—"

But Santiago had bounded up and begun tossing all his possessions into his portmanteau.

"Santo, it's a two-mile walk!"

"Do me good!"

She grinned. "*Bien.* Let's go home. I hate this place."

"I'll need help. Could you carry . . ." The thought of her carrying his portmanteau suddenly daunted him. "They'll send it over. If they don't I'll slap another warrant on someone."

He found his washed sheriff's clothes—white shirt, britches, and vest—and began tugging them on, pausing suddenly to let a faint spell pass. He undid his steel badge from his robe and pinned it back on his vest, feeling proud.

"You almost fainted."

"I'm going right now."

She caught his arm and led him to the cot and pulled him down beside her. "We'll make it, Santo. Let's go slowly."

"I can't stand this place."

"Are we going to tell Dr. Hoffmeister?"

"No. He's under orders to keep me here."

He stood slowly, feeling the blood leave his head. He eyed

his portmanteau and decided nothing important lay within it,
but he did pick up his medical valise. Twilight filtered through
the infirmary. The smells of evening mess, broth and bread,
lingered in the quiet wards. He walked resolutely through the
building and out into the soft, chill night, where aquamarine
light lingered in the west. As she walked silently beside him he
became conscious of the rustle of her skirts, and his thoughts
turned to things they hadn't shared for many weeks.

Fort Keogh seemed preternaturally quiet, abandoned. Lamplight glowed amber from a few windows in officers' quarters,
but the rest seemed dark and deserted. Maybe they all were out
on maneuvers or bivouac, or even tracking down another Sioux
village that had declined white man's hospitality. Santiago and
Mimi started down the familiar trail without being challenged.
After ten minutes his strength left him, and he sat down. She
sat beside him on the grasses.

"We're not even halfway, Santo."

Several soldiers emerged from the dusk, striding rapidly
toward Miles. He caught their laughter and thought perhaps
they had money in their britches. Payroll laughter. Mimi eased
her hand over to his medical valise, dug into it until she found
the Starr, and lifted it quietly into her lap.

"Mimi!" he whispered.

"Nothing's stopping us now," she replied.

Three enlisted men. No one he recognized.

"Evenin'," said one of them. "You taking the air?"

"Nice evening," said Santiago, watching them pass by.

A few minutes later two more loomed out of the night, and
when they drew close he recognized them. A sergeant and a
corporal. Two he'd never forget. Never. Both of them were
among the ones who'd pounded him to pulp, sent him to the
doors of death. He wished he had the Starr.

"Well, if it ain't the sheriff," said the sergeant. Buford.
"And his squaw."

"It's a good night for squawing," said the other.

Santiago stayed silent.

They didn't see his revolver snugged down in her lap. Nor
did it matter. The pair walked on toward town, laughing softly
in the dusk. His heart slowed, and he watched her slide the

weapon back into his valise. He let them get well ahead of him before he stood.

"Let's go, Mimi." He stood suddenly. "I want to get home so badly I can taste it."

"What does it taste like?"

"Like you," he said, laughing in the night.

"Now I know you're well," she said, tugging his arm closer.

The shots came muffled from ahead, three cracks, then a fourth. Then silence. Toole paused warily, his sheriff's instincts aroused. Maybe two hundred yards, three hundred, hard to tell. But not far. He paused.

"What is it?" she whispered.

"Nothing, I hope."

They walked quietly forward into deepening murk and almost stumbled on the first body, sprawled awkwardly across the trail. Buford. Santiago could see that. And beyond, the corporal. Alive moments ago; probably dead now.

"Santo!"

"Back, Mimi! The killer may still be here. Over there!" He waved her toward a cottonwood. But she didn't budge. She'd obviously had enough of running.

Sheriff and doctor fought in him. Sheriff won: He couldn't doctor until he knew he wouldn't be shot while doctoring. He stalked quietly in a large arc around the place, checking brush and hollows. Nothing. Halfway between Keogh and Miles. Nicely planned for an ambush. By day he might find some clues: heel prints, brass, hoof prints. But not now. Satisfied at last, he knelt over the sergeant and sought a pulse. Nothing. Blood glinted darkly in the starlight. He tried the other, found a wrist. No pulse. Both dead. Pockets of britches pulled out. Robbery? Payday. Maybe robbery by one of those footpads in town. Several of them came to mind.

Which way? Back to the Fort to report it? No, he'd act when he got to town.

"Mimi, we've got to report this to Wade."

"Leave them, Santo. Those were two of the ones who beat you. I despise them."

"I can't do that."

He hurried toward Miles, sensing her anger.

The other one, the corporal, was one of them. Both of them had helped at Hogtown. This was Sapp's work. Not robbery, but Sapp. Or someone hired by Sapp. It had started, then. He felt it in his bones. Sapp was lurking around here somewhere, systematically killing off the cabal who'd destroyed Hogtown—and him.

Toole felt an overpowering need to stop it. Stop the murder, even if murderer hunted murderer, killer stalked killer. Stop it in the name of justice and law. As soon as he got to Miles he'd head for the hotel and nab Sapp. Maybe he could save the rest of the cabal if he acted fast.

Chapter 17

Milestown roared. Santiago's route took them past the west-end saloons, gaudy with lantern light. Knots of soldiers caroused at every batwing door. From within, the scrape of fiddles and staccato laughter. Hundreds of soldiers; half the garrison or more, wandering from shadow to light, saloon to saloon. He caught glimpses of the hurdy-gurdy girls within, hearing their easy, husky laughter, and hurried Mimi past.

"Payday," she said, gawking at every bright interior. Outside, on Main Street, soldiers glimpsed his star and turned silent as he passed, eyeing Mimi curiously. Down on Sixth Street, red lanterns swung in the portals of the three houses there.

"Dangerous, Mimi." He hurried her along, wanting to shield her from these sights, feeling a sinking weariness that brought him close to collapse. The two dead men lay on his mind. He didn't know what to do about them.

"I know. But it doesn't look dangerous."

"Soldiers are paid to kill—and use force."

"That's what I heard."

He laughed shortly. They slid past the last of the saloons and into a deeper darkness engulfing the business block. The hotel. He steered her suddenly toward the Miles.

"Not now, Santo. Tomorrow. Tonight . . . you need rest. And I want to hold you. Just hold you."

He opened the battered door for her, and they entered the dim lobby, lit by a grudging lantern. No one. He banged the bell hard, and was rewarded at last by a rattle and rustle from somewhere in the bowels of the seedy building. Rutherford, of course. The bald man eyed them quizzically, half annoyed.

"You registering, Sheriff? I ain't seen you for . . . say, you out of the fort hospital?"

Rutherford eyed Mimi and glanced away. "We don't allow—" he began, and silenced himself.

"What room's Romanov in?" Toole asked curtly.

"That one? He checked out. Strange bugger."

"Where'd he go? He say anything?"

Rutherford peered at him from above gold-framed half glasses. "Now that one sure was a puzzle. No, he didn't say nothing. He had him a trap and dropped a bag in it and hied off. Livery stable trap. Just pulled out. At least he let me know; not like that drummer Quigby who just pulled out with nary a word. They shared a room, y'know. The drummer and that Rooshan seer or whatever he was."

"I don't know. I have business with them both, Rutherford."

"I bet you do, Sheriff. Never liked the looks of that Rooshan. The other, the fat drummer, he seemed a pleasant one. In fact, I got all mixed up. The big one came first, registered as Januarius Quigby. Then the fat drummer came, said he was Quigby and the other was his brother. Then he vanished and the big one signs himself Romanov. Stayed in his room until I wondered how the man even ate, staying in like that. Only lately he's taken to galavanting around. Got him a hat to cover up some strange jewelry he got pinned to his head. Never saw that before, head jewelry. I'd think someone would rob him, yank his hair off for it."

Santiago absorbed all that while paging through the register. He found the Romanov signature, Teaneck, New Jersey. Then he paged some more and found the Quigby signature, weeks earlier. Same handwriting.

"Rutherford, can you think of anything else about this Quigby?"

"Darned if I can. Hardly remember him. Brown eyes, I guess, sort of out of focus. *He* was out of focus, that's the best way to tell of it. Upped and left. He sold apothecary goods."

"He did? What kind?"

"Nothing I ever heard of."

"Rutherford, I'd like to look at that room."

"Sorry, Sheriff. It's been cleaned and rented out to some ranch woman in for shopping. Deaf as a stone. I have to yell at her to make her understand."

Santiago sighed, exhausted. "Well, thanks, Rutherford."

"Them two wanted men?"

Santiago smiled. "Let me know if you see either one."

The darkness outside embraced them. A sharp, premonitory cold lay in the air.

"I've got to do something about those dead men," he muttered.

"Santo, they've been discovered by now—all those soldiers in town, going back. . . ."

He headed grimly toward the livery barn, finding it dark. But he knew where he'd find old Blue. He rattled the door of the office and presently a match flared within, and lantern light glowed from beneath the door. Blue—no one knew him by any more name that that—poked his head out, yawning. The night hostler wore only his red longjohns, stained black from half a year's wear.

"You," he said, stifling a yawn.

"Blue. I've got urgent business. I want you to drive a wagon out the fort road. About halfway, there's two soldiers . . . on the ground. Want you to pick them up and take them to Keogh. Tell them I sent you."

Blue's better eye widened. "Them two is drunk?"

"Dead."

"Do it yerself, damn ye."

Toole sighed. "I'll come with you. Too tired to help lift, though."

"No, Santo!"

He clasped an arm around Mimi. "Just take an hour. I'll be in the wagon, getting rest."

"You can hardly stand up!" Mimi protested.

He didn't argue that.

"I ain't pickin' up bodies! Anyways, I belong here for customers!" Blue glared fiercely at him.

"Harness a wagon, Blue. Bill it to the county."

Ten minutes later Sheriff Toole found himself driving west from Milestown into the night. Alone. It'd taken his remaining strength to talk Mimi into waiting at home. The lurch of the wagon kept him from falling asleep, a need in him so overpowering he gauged his whole mission in terms of staying awake.

Ahead he spotted a bobbing lantern and shadowed men, and as he pulled up he found himself staring into the faces of half a dozen soldiers. The one holding the lantern eyed him, his star, and the wagon. A cavalry man, yellow stripe down his britches.

"Good," said Toole. "Load them in here for me."

"You that sheriff in the post infirmary?"

"Toole. Yes. I was. You know anything about how this happened?"

"I was fixing to ask you that, Sheriff."

"I found them earlier. Load 'em up now. You know their names?"

"Buford and LeMat."

He watched them lift the two bodies and settle them in the wagon box.

"You're a doctor, aren't ya?" asked the trooper. "How come you ain't even having a look?"

"I already looked. They were dead," Toole replied wearily. "I'm tired. You want to drive, Trooper?"

"Beats walking, even with a load like that." The man clambered up, and rolled the wagon toward Keogh. Behind, men stared.

"It was robbery, I think. See them pockets out, Sheriff?"

"I did," he muttered.

Santiago wobbled and dozed on his seat, until the wagon halted suddenly before the night guardroom.

Within minutes he found himself surrounded by Colonel Wade, Dr. Hoffmeister, and two lieutenants, variously half-dressed or in robes. All gaping at him, at the bodies, at the star glinting on his black vest.

"I suppose I should have a talk with you, Toole," said Wade.

"I suppose you should."

"You leave the infirmary without authorization and secretly. And you come back with two bodies. Men whose identity you've mentioned to me for certain reasons."

"I'm a civilian and a sheriff and a doctor," Toole replied sharply.

"I suppose it's all a coincidence."

Santiago sighed. The colonel would be a blockhead to the last. "If you're saying I left the hospital to murder these two, Colonel . . ."

"No, no. It's just a coincidence that seems strange."

"I told you who would do it. And who would be on his list, Colonel. I looked for him tonight—he'd been at the hotel under a false name. Now he's gone. Probably out to his new place. The new dive. Where I intend to go in the morning."

"We'll cooperate. Send along some support for you."

Toole shook his head. "You still don't understand. I'm investigating some of your men. I'm investigating Sapp. I'll do it alone, I'm sworn to defend law and justice, not the army. If you want to help, throw Wiltz in the guardhouse. I think the others still alive are named Liggett and Polanc."

"Why . . . I couldn't do that."

"Suit yourself, Colonel. I'll arrest them anyway."

"By God, Sheriff, if I weren't taking heat from a bunch of public officials, I'd—"

From the darkness Mrs. LeMat emerged, weeping. "Let me see him. Oh, God . . ." The woman stared, sobbed, and collapsed, sinking to the parade beside the wagon. "Len, Len, Len," she wailed. "Len, Len, Len . . ."

Santiago watched helplessly, not without bitterness. If Wade had cooperated, and not covered things up . . . but no. If that had happened Mrs. LeMat would be weeping before jailbars or the gallows instead of this wagon box. He sighed. Never had he dealt with a case like this, with victims and the guilty all one and the same. Holy Mary, where was right?

From out of the darkness rose a new wail, cold as death, and another weeping woman stumbled into the lantern light. "Help me!" she cried. "It's my mister, Mr. Polanc. In the privy."

He awakened to the subtle scent of Earl Gray tea in his nostrils. She sat on the edge of the bed, holding a tray with the blue Wedgwood teapot and cups on it. The brown light lit her face, accentuating her honeyed flesh and the large cheekbones of her mother's people. The whiteness of her high-necked nightgown always did that, honeyed her flawless flesh and built a need in him.

"An hour!" she said. "It was three hours, and then Adelbert Hoffmeister had to drive you home and help you in. You were beyond scolding, so he scolded me." She smiled. "You don't even remember it, Santo. You were asleep on your feet."

She kissed him softly, scraping her lips over his beard stubble, and then poured. "I held you all night. And then I let you sleep late."

He accepted the cup and saucer. No use talking until he had tea in him. Anything before tea would be addled. He sipped, reading the music of her eyes without talking. She was bursting with things to say, and waiting for his tea to take hold. Her expression slid from inscrutable to indignant, and he saw French on her lips though she said nothing.

"I'm going to go with you," she said after his fifth sip.

"What are you talking about, Mimi?"

"What you're planning to do today."

"It's dangerous."

"That's why I'm going."

"No. You could make me vulnerable."

"Maybe. I could also save your life. When I shoot I aim and squeeze and my spirit is cold. My mother is an expert torturer. Especially of Crows. She cuts off fingers and toes joint by joint. And other things. She jabs slivers of pitch pine into Crow flesh. Sioux, too, and ignites them. But that's nothing compared to what she does with Blackfeet. Do you want to hear it?"

"You shock me."

"I'm worse than my mother. It's the French in me. I can do it smiling."

"You're a savage."

"That's what you always say in the middle of passion."

"You're French."

"That's what you always say before passion."

"I don't suppose I can keep you here."

"No. You need protecting. You will do this thing because you're stubborn and Irish and full of notions. Any Frenchman, like my father, would shrug and say let the evil ones destroy each other. Let this Sapp kill the army murderers; let the army destroy the wicked Sapp. Justice would be done even if you didn't lift a finger.''

"I could do that."

"But you won't, Santo."

She was right. He scarcely knew why he pursued the matter. Everything about it had become tangled. Victims were killers and slavers; killers were victims. Murder had been done to men who deserved it. Then he thought of China Belle, who hadn't deserved it—hadn't deserved Sapp's slavery or an army bullet. He'd go to the new Hogtown today because of her and the other slaves; because the law said murder is a crime in its own right, regardless of who was murdered; because men in the army had no more right to murder than civilians. Because an impartial civil trial of the survivors, Sapp and any new accomplice of his, Wiltz, Liggett, would answer the cry of justice. . . .

But mostly because he'd grown stubborn. He'd been kicked and pounded to the brink of death; defied. His evidence stolen. His wife—ah, lady—insulted and gravely jeopardized. His office and oath treated lightly. His duties mocked. Criminals ran loose, and if he didn't stop them they'd do worse. He'd pinch Sapp, and stop the current wave of murder. Then he'd deal with Wiltz somehow, someway. That was the Irish in him, and now he let it run his blood, course through him until he felt reckless and heady with it, with his Irish flintiness.

"I know what I'm going to do," he said softly. "My father said if you must do something on principle, be sure to do it or it'll eat you up."

"The Irish are crazy. The French are more practical."

"If I'm crazy, it's for a cause. I have to do it, Mimi."

"Oh, Santo. I know. But I wish . . ."

"I am going to arrest armed men," he said. He set down his teacup and folded her to him, sliding his hand over honeyed flesh under the cotton.

"Santo—when this is done, would you resign? You're a doctor. You should be healing people—not this. . . ."

A racket at the front door interrupted. He sighed, irritably. "Sheriff or doctor, sheriff or doctor," he muttered, releasing her. She looked upset.

Sylvane Tobias stood outside.

"I knew you were back. I didn't expect to see you again."

"I didn't expect to see you either, Sylvane. Did you recover? I still plan to arrest Wiltz."

"Took a week. You still down, or you up and about now?"

"I do what's necessary."

"Well, Toole, there's another one in my icehouse. A stranger fished out of the river by some Sioux early this morning, two, three miles below town, I gather. Awfullest throat wound I ever did see. They found some of his clothes on the bank, half mile above."

Santiago dressed, donning his black worsted britches, white collarless shirt, and black vest. In a few minutes he stood in the blue gloom of the icehouse, beside a diminished mound covered with sawdust. A pudgy man lay on the cold shelf of ice, his brown suit still dripping water. His throat had been torn out of him, making a ghastly hole. Tooth marks peppered his jowly flesh around the wound. A lash of some sort had cut his flesh.

"Nothing in his pockets," said Sylvane. "You any idea who he is?"

"Yes," said Santiago. "Sylvane—that throat and those marks. What do they suggest to you?"

"Bites. Catamount, maybe. Doesn't look like fish, not with those tooth holes. A coyote got him after he died?"

"No, a wolf killed him."

"How do you know that? Who is he?" Sylvane stared at him skeptically.

"Sylvane, this is what I need! This man was murdered; I know the killer and I know the weapon, which the killer still has."

Santiago undid the man's shirt, looking for bullet holes, and found none. But lower down, below the sternum—a stab wound, small.

"I'll be durned," said Sylvane.

"I think I know this weapon, too. Something to watch out for. Sylvane, this is a big break for me. Could you run some errands? First, I need old Rutherford to make an identification. Next, I need Huffman, at the photographic studio. I'll have him take some photos of this neck wound. Those Sioux—they around?"

"Nope. They was plumb scared they'd be accused of it and beat it. I got a little of it with sign language, sort of. They pointed down the river some, showed me the clothing. I got it here."

Santiago went through it, finding nothing in the soggy mass. "Whoever killed him was careful. Nothing."

"Toole, you're plumb being mysterious on me."

"I'll explain later, Sylvane. If you'll fetch Huffman and his equipment, I'll go find Rutherford."

In ten minutes, he had assembled them all in the gloomy icehouse.

"That's him—Quigby. That's the one. I can tell, even with all those teeth marks. Ain't he like I said, sort of soft and hard to describe?"

"Januarius Quigby. The one who registered?"

"No, dammit, his brother. I could never get that straightened out. The other's Romanov."

"Actually, Rutherford, this is Quigby. He's a drummer, maybe. I suspect he was other things." He stared at them all. "I may need you as witnesses in court. Please observe that throat wound and the tooth marks, and this belly wound. Now, Mr. Huffman, I need at least four pictures."

"Outside in the sun, Sheriff."

They carried the body into a weak sun, and Huffman set up his tripod and plates and took a photograph from each side, and one straight on. The final plate was a close-up of the belly wound with a ruler placed next to it.

"Do I bill the county or you?"

"I was fixing to ask the same thing," said Tobias.

"Custer County. They'll fight it. I'll insist."

He stared once more at the body, wondering if he'd done everything. Four witnesses of its condition. Photographs. Not yet decomposed . . . but soon.

"Bury him, Sylvane. In canvas. If he's what I think, that's decent enough. If he's a better man, then God forgive me."

Evidence at last. Sapp had eluded him for years, but no longer. Maybe this would be a lever he could use to pry more from the man. Luck of the Irish, he thought. Go do what you have to, and the means will follow.

Chapter 18

The telegraph man handed Sergeant Major Vernon Wiltz a yellow flimsy with block letters printed on it.

"This is for the colonel," he said.

Wiltz nodded and spread the sheet before him. It was addressed to Colonel Orville Prescott Wade, CO, Fort Keogh, Department of Dakota, and dated August 31, 1880.

> ALL ENLISTED PERSONNEL ACCUSED OF ALLEGED CRIMES AGAINST CIVILIANS ARE SUBJECT TO COURT-MARTIAL ACCORDING TO UNIFORM MILITARY CODE. NO CIVILIAN SHALL BE DETAINED OR TRIED BY MILITARY EXCEPT UNDER SPECIAL CIRCUMSTANCES. ADHERE STRICTLY. SHERMAN.

The sergeant smiled. So much for Sheriff Toole's snares. There'd been an uproar in Washington City and Helena. That was plain enough. But old Three Mugs Wade had had his wings clipped slightly. "Adhere strictly" was shorthand no army man could miss. Wiltz rose, stretched on the balls of his feet, feeling just fine, and entered Wade's office without knocking.

"Yes?" snapped the CO, looking up from *Harper's* magazine.

"Telegram from General Sherman, sah."

The colonel studied the flimsy, ire reddening his ivory flesh. "That's it. Throws it all in my lap." He glared at Wiltz. "I'll get to the bottom of this thing right now. I've three men murdered—all of them named to me by Sheriff Toole. He told me their life was threatened—and he told me why." Wade glared at him. "Two apparently robbed of payday money, but that means nothing. The other stabbed in his outhouse at night. All within an hour. Horn's gone. That leaves you and Liggett. Get Liggett. Requisition two cavalry mounts and have my own gelding saddled. We're riding to Hogtown in ten minutes."

"Sah, there's no need to involve yourself. . . ."

Wade stood slowly, leaking rage from every pore. "Sergeant Major Wiltz. You will follow orders without a word. One word and you are no longer a sergeant major."

Wiltz's instinct was to crush the bug before him with a swift uppercut to the solar plexus. "Very good, sah."

He wheeled out smartly, found Liggett instructing ten new men in unjamming the trapdoor Springfield. "Corporal, you're posted to special duty. You men—attach yourself to Corporal Hintz over there this morning."

He led Liggett toward the stables, explaining as they walked. "We're ordered to go with the CO to Hogtown at once."

Liggett stared sharply. "There? With him? I've been waiting for a bullet in me all morning. That's half the reason I'm working with rifles now. Do you believe it—that Sapp's alive and he's after us?"

"Don't know what to believe. I'm thinking Sapp's brother or friend or something like that, someone getting even," Wiltz said. "Get the colonel's horse saddled, and two for us. I'm getting shotguns. He didn't request arms, but I'm not going in there unarmed. Sawed-off, double-barreled ten-gauge, with buckshot and sidearms. That teaches respect."

"What'll happen, Sergeant?"

"Cheer up, Max. We'll have a look and know what to burn—and who—later. Stroke of luck." Wiltz laughed easily, humor racing through his thick frame and bull neck.

"Maybe we're dead, Sarge."

"Did it ever occur to you that colonels ain't bulletproof, Liggett? I tried to keep him from going. Adjutant probably heard me; he hears everything in there. One last thing, Liggett. Don't sing songs. Be careful. And ask permission to speak. He's a little techy this mornin'."

Minutes later Colonel Wade was leading the other two horsemen upriver from Keogh under an autumnal, herringbone sky, along the foot of the river bluff, on a trail better known to hundreds of enlisted men than officers.

They rounded the last hump of land and turned up the long coulee. Before them the place glowed, whitewashed or calcimined so that it jolted the eye even under the overcast. Several drays sagged in front, and Wiltz could see roustabouts and teamsters from Miles wrestling heavy tables covered with green baize up the stoop. Two women lounged in wrappers on the porch, their hair dyed unnatural colors like the leaves of autumn. From within, even on that gray day, lamplight gilded green and white things.

"Hogtown?" Wade said.

"Permission to speak, sah. The old place was logs, sod roof, dirt floor, smelled like piss and vomit. So dark a man could hardly find the doll picking his pocket."

Wade nodded. "All right. Don't think I haven't observed your shotguns. We won't have an incident. I'm rather happy you brought them, but if you use them without my express permission or command . . ." He left the rest unsaid. Wiltz understood and didn't give a damn. If it came to blowing buckshot into someone about to kill him, he'd risk the court-martial. He glanced at Liggett and saw a similar sentiment in the corporal's eyes, and a bitter smile. There are ways to countermand orders, and the world will never find out, Wiltz thought, eyeing the colonel's ramrod blue back.

They dismounted at a shining new hitchrail and climbed the steps, the wood echoing under their boots. Workmen paid no attention.

"Some Hogtown," said Liggett.

The colonel glared at him.

Within the double doors everything dazzled, from white walls to crystal chandelier with two of its lamps lit. One thing dominated. Before them, high on the wall, a huge painting of a nude, perhaps twelve feet by six, in an ornate gilded frame. No ordinary smiling, dimpled, fleshy nude with a diaphanous fig leaf, but a slender one with an unsmiling visage, and posed lewdly. Wade stared, and glanced covertly at three smiling women.

"Advertisement," said Wiltz.

"Well. Yes." Colonel Wade peered sharply about, finally settling on one of the women, a buxom blonde.

"Where's the proprietor?" he asked.

"Why, dearie, he's around. We haven't opened yet, but if we can be of service . . ."

Liggett laughed and Wade's glare withered him.

"Who owns it?"

"I'm not sure, honey. I think Romanov. There was another one, Quigby. He's not around. But Cottonmouth is."

"Maybe Toole didn't know what he was talking about," Wade muttered. "Who's Cottonmouth, ma'am?"

"Manager. He'll run the bank and the bar and all that."

"I'm Cottonmouth." The whispery voice came from the corridor plunging toward the rear. A skeletal man lounged against the door frame, eyeing them with ice eyes. Revolvers nestled in low-slung holsters on his black britches.

Wiltz swung the shotgun nestled in the crook of his arm around, while Cottonmouth watched and grinned. "You're dead," he whispered.

Wade puffed up slowly until the double row of brass buttons down the chest of his tunic seemed to radiate the lamplight, and the gold-threaded epaulets of rank to pop off his shoulders. "I'm looking for a man called Sapp," he said curtly. "I'm Colonel Wade, commander at Fort Keogh."

"Never heard of Sapp. Oh, I guess I have. Didn't he die in Hogtown when Wiltz and this fellow here—Liggett—shot them all?"

Wade's pupils contracted oddly, and then dilated.

It might be, thought Vernon Wiltz, that some powder would burn this gray morning. Some of the workmen paused to watch, while others wrestled the green-topped tables into place. Wiltz spotted others now, sporting men, foreigners to sunlight, standing pale about the shining bar, reflected in the mirrored back bar. Some operation here. No Hogtown, but a sin palace intended to suck every nickel from the army.

"Fetch the proprietor, man. Tell him it's Wade of the United States Army."

Cottonmouth shuffled indolently, smiled, and nodded. He

vanished down the dark corridor, deliberately turning his white-shirted back to them.

Wade turned to Wiltz. "I always emphasize the army. They know what the army can do to a dump like this. A single order of mine can put it off limits. Some palace. Utterly beyond the imagination of a swine like Sapp and his dram shop. Toole had it wrong. Bullheaded, stupid sheriff. . . ."

Wiltz nodded, keeping a sharp eye on the sports along the bar. Liggett was sweating like a cold beer in July, great black patches under his armpits. He'd gripped his shotgun in a ready position, and was studying the sports feverishly.

Wiltz smiled at him. "Cottonmouth," he said. "And the owner."

Liggett nodded.

They heard a thumping in the corridor, slow and halting; a scrape and a cane. Then a tall, gaunt man limped into the white and gilt room, a bearded man wearing a black derby and an immaculate swallowtail coat of gray. A stranger, yet vaguely familiar, who stirred unaccustomed anxieties in Wiltz. A weak man, though; no match for a fist or shotgun. But beside the man, Popskull. And behind, in the darkness, the one called Cottonmouth.

"Romanov at your service," the man said. His eyes, though, settled on Wiltz. Familiar eyes, brown like Sapp's. He grinned faintly. The yellow-eyed wolf trotted boldly forward, occupying the no-man's-land between them all.

"Well, Romanov," Wade began in a stentorian roar that seemed to rattle the windows, "we're investigating crimes. Two of my men robbed and murdered and another stabbed in his privy, all in the space of an hour. I'm here to inform you that everyone here is suspect, and I'll get to the bottom of it."

Romanov smiled. "Buford, LeMat, and Polanc. Three of the ones who burnt Hogtown and slaughtered them all. I see two more right there. But not Horn. You shipped him out, did you?"

Wiltz stared uneasily. The colonel's ivory flesh froze to his cheekbones. "Strange allegations. Nonsense. You have some nefarious purpose, you and Sheriff Toole."

But Romanov's gaze had abandoned the colonel, as if the colonel's words were unimportant. Instead, he focused on

Wiltz, smiling, and slowly lifted a hand to his derby and doffed it. The blaze of gold over his right ear blistered Wiltz's vision. Vernon Wiltz gaped. Slowly, the man settled the derby back over his gaunt head. Could it be? Impossible! He didn't even look like Sapp. And yet . . . the wolf. The right height, right eyes, right tone of voice. A cold, mean joy flowed through Sergeant Wiltz, blood pumping through the machinery of his body, blood out to the levers and hammers, mauls and axes, drills and battering rams of his limbs.

Wiltz glanced briefly at Liggett, who looked terror-stricken and trigger-crazy. Somehow that wraith of a Cottonmouth had slid out and a quarter-circle away from Sapp or Romanov, and stood under the mesmerizing nude.

"What's that on your head?" asked Wade.

"My crown jewels."

Wiltz could not look at Cottonmouth without noticing the nude, which sucked his gaze upward.

Wade stabbed a gloved finger at Romanov. "You. You've accused some of my men of misconduct. What evidence have you? I'm here to get to the bottom of this, and now's your chance."

Romanov smiled quietly. "I saw it all. About one, after a slow night. Everyone here in bed. Quiet, efficient, and fast. Wiltz there shot Sapp while he lay abed. Horn, he shot the poxy kid, but the kid shot him in the arm. Liggett there shot two bar men, Bull Jarvis and Milo Dansk. Wiltz there shot the dollies, I think. I didn't see that. Big Lulu, Little Etta, Cheyenne Rose, China Belle, Bigmouth Lilly. Tossed them in a common grave—you can see the remains of it out there—and burnt everything."

Wade looked testy. "Romanov, I asked for proof, not a story. Who are you and how came you to witness all this?"

From without, the soft clop of hooves and hiss of buggy wheels drifted to them. Wiltz scarcely dared take his eyes off Cottonmouth. Voices then, familiar voices. A woman's exclamations. Feet on stairs. In the wide double doors, against the blinding light, the silhouettes of a man and woman, Toole and his wife.

*   *   *

"Santo, look at that woman!" Mimi exclaimed.

"Mimi . . . you'd better wait. . . . This isn't a place . . ." Santiago, his eyes adjusting to the gilded gloom, studied them all. "Amazing," he muttered. His gaze rested sharply on Wiltz, then Sapp, then the curled-up wolf, then Cottonmouth, and then swiftly the sports and slatterns lining the bar. Then, more carefully, he studied the two sawed-off double-barreled shotguns, Cottonmouth's weaponry, and the alert wolf. He didn't miss Sapp's deadly walking stick, either.

"A welcome surprise. Colonel. Sapp. Sergeant." He gazed at Cottonmouth. "I've seen you in Bug's but I have no name for you."

Cottonmouth grinned.

"You called that man there Sapp!" Wade exclaimed.

"Mordecai Sapp. I treated him that night and put the gold in his head to seal the bullet holes in his skull. Lift that derby, Sapp. I see rearranging your brain didn't improve your appetite any."

The man guffawed.

"You shot him in the head but didn't kill him, Wiltz. You buried him shallow, gave up the job when the deluge started, and his wolf there and a flash flood released him. He was covered with mud when he arrived, but alive, Wiltz, alive to tell tales."

He watched Sergeant Major Vernon Wiltz absorb that and swing the barrels of his shotgun halfway toward him, menacing him. A bluff, thought Santiago. Wiltz knew where the first shot would come from, if it got down to shooting.

He sensed Mimi separating from him, gliding closer to Cottonmouth. He dreaded that something might happen to her, and yet he found her a comfort. He glanced and saw her digging in her reticule, and knew her fingers were closing around the cold, hard grip of her small revolver.

"Mr. Sapp," he continued. "I've come to pinch you for murder."

Sapp looked surprised, and smiled faintly. "You're mixing up medicine and law. The last I knew, Wiltz and Liggett there tried to murder me, shot me, half buried me, killed my people, and burnt my business."

"We found Quigby, Sapp. Killed by two weapons still in your possession. I've had Huffman photograph the wounds for the court. Will you come along peaceably?"

Sapp's gaze darted about, assessing things.

"Resisting arrest is itself a crime, Sapp. A lot of witnesses here."

Sapp did nothing.

"Colonel Wade, what's the pay of a corporal? And a buck sergeant?"

"Why . . . seventeen and twenty dollars."

"How is your payroll disbursed—specie?"

"No, bills here. Some other places gold or silver. But it came in greenbacks this time. Small denominations, of course."

Toole turned to Cottonmouth. "You. Empty your pockets. Slowly now."

Cottonmouth grinned and did nothing.

"I think, young fellow, you don't want to empty them."

Cottonmouth whispered. "I own a lot more than thirty-seven dollars, Toole."

"I'm sure you do. Sapp paid you well for killing Buford, LeMat, and Polanc."

Wade's eyes dilated and his jowl twitched. Vernon Wiltz stared, snaked-eyed, at Cottonmouth. He glanced at Liggett, whose shotgun had pivoted toward Cottonmouth. Wiltz smiled.

"You got no proof, Sheriff."

"You'll have thirty-seven dollars in small bills, and maybe much more in your pockets."

"Maybe you'll have to make me do it."

Cottonmouth grinned languorously, his white hands not far from his revolvers.

Toole didn't like it. Four deadly men, and he wanted them all for murder, if he could somehow keep them from blowing each other apart and keep them from turning on him.

"We'll assist you, Sheriff," said Colonel Wade. "Men, prepare yourselves."

"No, Colonel, I'll handle this," said Toole blandly. "I'll be arresting Wiltz and Liggett for murder, along with Sapp and Cottonmouth."

"You can't, Toole. I have orders from Washington. I'll not

release my men to you. If there's a trial of a man under arms, it'll be a court-martial.''

Toole nodded. He'd been afraid of that, and supposed Wiltz and Liggett would get off. For an instant he felt blind rage: He couldn't touch the man who'd almost murdered him twice. He studied Wiltz and saw mockery there, the look of a man beyond his reach. Very well then, he thought. That makes Wiltz and Liggett allies of sorts. They want Sapp and this other albino one as badly as the law does.

He addressed Cottonmouth. "You. Unbuckle that belt of yours, slowly.''

"You going to try me, Sheriff?'' The man stood easily beneath the nude, his ghostly hands poised inches from the grips of his revolvers.

Along the bar, sports and dollies scrambled, some ducking behind it, others fleeing the room. Santiago glanced at them.

"Now see here, Toole,'' said Colonel Wade. "That man there looks to be one of those fast-shooting men. You're being a bit bullheaded.'' He motioned to Wiltz. "Sergeant! Assist the sheriff here with your shotgun.''

"Begging your pardon, Sah, but—''

Cottonmouth's hands blurred, lifting blue metal. Black bores erupted powder smoke in a single instant. A roar insulted Santiago's ears. He saw red blossom on Wiltz's left shoulder, spoiling Wiltz's aim as the shotgun roared. The blast of buckshot blew the nude's belly out.

Santiago pulled his Starr, watching Wiltz and Sapp. Especially Wiltz.

Cottonmouth smiled. Santiago glimpsed Liggett tumbling to earth, a hole in his forehead. Liggett's shotgun clattered on the planks. Wiltz pulled the other trigger and buckshot belched toward Sapp but went high, blowing his derby off and shattering bar glasses. Sapp's skull-gold shone. Another of Cottonmouth's bullets struck Wiltz in the lower ribs.

"Stop this at once!'' Wade yelled.

"Go, Popskull!'' Sapp cried in a strange, high voice. The wolf glanced at the pointed finger and catapulted toward Wiltz, open-jawed. Santiago's shot caught it midair, through the chest. The wolf's momentum plunged it into Wiltz, its jaws snapping. Wiltz staggered, dropped his empty shotgun, and drew his revolver.

Sapp plunged a hand into his gray swallowtail and pulled a hideout gun, a four-barreled pepperbox. Another of Cottonmouth's bullets pierced Wiltz's right leg just as Wiltz kicked the snarling, rolling wolf. Cottonmouth surveyed his work and turned toward Toole, the last of his targets.

Mimi steadied her revolver, aimed carefully, and shot Cottonmouth through the side of the head. Cottonmouth eyed her, astonished, and folded to earth, leaking blood. Mimi muttered to herself. Wiltz howled happily. He whirled and emptied the Colt into Sapp, who caved toward the floor with red-blooming holes in his neck, right chest, and jaw, bloodying the swallowtail. His spasming fingers fired the pepperbox, perforating the nude's right breast.

From behind the bar women screamed.

"Santo, I killed him," she snapped. "Now I'll scalp him."

"A savage!" cried Colonel Wade.

"On both sides, French and Assiniboin," she said.

Sapp clambered to his feet, blood gouting from several places, limped forward with a macabre gloat on his face, rapping his walking stick, and then thrust it at Wiltz. Toole shot Sapp in the chest. The blade sliced through Wiltz's blouse but then the walking stick fell from Sapp's hand, clattering on the bloody planks. Sapp folded and rolled onto his back, sighing.

Wiltz laughed and plucked Liggett's shotgun from the floor, then fired at Colonel Wade, who was dancing about yelling "Stop!"

Wade staggered back, gasping, with some buckshot pellets in the side of the chest. The blast at Wade stunned Santiago, and suddenly he knew he'd be next. Wiltz lifted the shotgun toward Toole and started to squeeze, but a bullet from Santiago's Starr pierced the palm of his hand. The shotgun clattered onto the planks, one barrel still smoking.

Cottonmouth crawled toward one of his revolvers. Toole shot him. Cottonmouth collapsed again, a giggle dying in his throat.

The wolf, still alive and leaking gore, sprang at Wiltz, clamping its jaws over the sergeant's throat. Wiltz wrestled

with the blood-soaked animal. Santiago aimed carefully, and
shot. The wolf spasmed and slowly went limp, falling at
Wiltz's feet.

"Stop! I say stop!" cried Wade, clutching his bloody side.
"Holy Mary!" cried Toole.

Chapter 19

Always, the sheriffing came before the doctoring, a thing that Santiago sometimes resented. But it couldn't be helped. He stood, reloading his Starr carefully, studying the smoked place.

"Help me, Toole. I'm shot!" muttered Colonel Wade.

"In a moment, Colonel. I have to secure things first, or there might not be a doc to treat you."

From the floor, Wiltz stared at Toole grayly, blood leaking from five holes in his massive frame. He grinned, a deathly gleam in his eye.

From behind the bar sports and ladies fearfully emerged, standing up, gaping at twitching bodies. From behind the gaming tables teamsters and roustabouts slowly rose, looking ready to dive again.

Santiago liked the looks of one, young and fearless. "You, I'm deputizing you." He picked up Liggett's shotgun, dug through Liggett's pockets for shells, and reloaded. "Here now. Take this and keep it on those sports. No one leaves here. I want statements from you all."

The young man accepted the weapon with a nod and swiveled it casually around. Mimi returned from outside, carrying his medical valise.

"Good, Mimi. Reload and watch."

She nodded.

Decisions. Wiltz bled from a wound below the right shoulder, the lower rib cage, his hand, an arm, and his thigh. The thigh wound pumped bright blood through the hole in his britches. The femoral artery.

179

"Wiltz, pull your belt and make a tourniquet. You"—he pointed at a teamster—"help him. Tight. At the groin."

The man obeyed. Santiago turned to Colonel Wade. He didn't like Wade, but he cared less about Wiltz. Decisions. He took the colonel's pulse. Fast and weak. Shock, or near it.

"I can barely breathe. Paralyzed," muttered Wade. Santiago eased the man's tunic off and then cut away the blue blouse and the white linens, stained bright red. Two holes in the man's left side. A furrow where a third ball had plowed across ribs and caromed off the sternum. Wade panted, sighing.

"I need a lamp, Mimi, please."

She looked around helplessly, until the deputized teamster lifted one from the chandelier. Santiago peered into the bloody holes. One hole yielded nothing. The other one, bleeding less hard, revealed a ball, gray and bloody against ribs.

"You're lucky, Colonel, so far."

He found some forceps in his kit, dipped them in carbolic, and extracted the flattened ball. Wade groaned.

"Hang on, Colonel. I'll have an anodyne in a while."

"Hurry, Toole!"

He slapped a plaster over the hole, which had begun to bleed copiously after he'd removed the ball. The other hole, back toward the spine, looked worse. Tender red pulp, no sign of anything in it, and bleeding steadily.

"I'm going to have to probe," he said. "And you'll have to hang on."

Wade nodded grayly.

Santiago slid long-jawed forceps into the hole, deeper and deeper, while Wade groaned. Santiago's hopes sank with each fraction of an inch. The wound ran along the ribs as they curved into the spine.

"Jesus!" cried Wade.

The probe touched something solid, metal or bone. He rotated the instrument gently. Wade sweated. The ball lay in there, very close to the spinal column. He pulled the probe out and used his fingers, finding the lump back from the entry hole. He made up his mind in an instant. He'd cut. He fished for the carbolic and wiped it generously over the flesh and the entry hole.

"Wade, I have to cut this one out."

The colonel nodded. "Hurry. My lungs don't work right."

He found his scalpel, dipped it in carbolic, and incised over the lump. Blood spurted. He cut again, until the blade struck metal. Then with his small forceps he plucked the ball out.

"Out. Lucky, Wade. Neither one in your chest cavity. This'll hurt."

He dabbed carbolic in the wound. Wade gasped.

"Hold this pad, Wade, hold it tight. I'll look to Wiltz."

"Laudanum, Toole!"

"No, you're in shock, or on the edge. Later." He covered Wade with his tunic to keep him warm.

What was there about medicine he found so satisfying? He'd probably saved Wade. Sheriffing, doctoring, madness. One of Wiltz's wounds, through the palm, he'd put there. Offices. Shoot them as sheriff, and then doctor them. He stared at Wiltz with loathing, not wanting to repair a murderer, the killer most likely of China Belle, and God knows how many others.

"Sometimes, Wiltz, I wish a patient would relieve me of responsibility."

"I ain't dead yet, Toole. Five holes and I'll make it."

"I'll save you for the firing squad."

Wiltz guffawed.

He liked sheriffing, too. As sheriff he freed the community of its violent diseases, as antiseptically as carbolic killed bacteria. He glanced at the three sprawled bodies. Cottonmouth, with a single hole through his head. Mimi's work. Liggett, a blue hole in his forehead, Cottonmouth's work. Sapp, perforated all over, Wiltz's work and his own coup de grace.

He cut away Wiltz's pant leg. Entrance and exit, clean wound, leaking blood slowly now that the teamster held the tourniquet. He doubted a plaster would stop the hemorrhage.

"Mimi, please start heating that knife blade. Take the chimney off the lamp."

He turned to the other wounds.

One pierced through lower left ribs, exited near the thoracic vertebrae. Not bleeding much. One through flesh of the upper left arm, entrance and exit clean, leaking blood. One just above his rib cage on left. No exit. Lodged against the scapula in there. He jabbed carbolic into the arm wound and wrapped it hard, stopped the sheeting blood.

"You've got a bullet lodged against your shoulder bone. Maybe Dr. Hoffmeister can dig it out."

"I don't die easy, Toole."

"Then you'll enjoy the noose all the less."

The lower wound he couldn't tell about. Diaphragm, probably above the stomach and spleen. "Hurt when you breathe?"

"Yes."

"Can you move your toes?"

"Yes."

"You're lucky."

One more wound, in the hand. Shattered metacarpal bones, limited use in the future.

Mimi handed him the heated knife. He took it by its handle, carefully. "Hope it's hot enough," he muttered. "Wiltz, this will be worse than anything you've ever experienced. And I've got to do it twice." He beckoned to the teamster. "Hold him."

He pressed the flat of the blade over the thigh wound, frying the flesh beneath. Wiltz howled. Smoke curled upward, and the stink of scorched tissue. He handed the blade back to Mimi, who heated it in the lantern flame again while Wiltz blubbered crazily. They rolled Wiltz on his side to get to the exit hole at the back of his thigh, and this time the hot blade ripped a shriek from him, and more babbling. Santiago inspected the cauterized holes, and beckoned the teamster to loosen the tourniquet. The burnt flesh and blood held.

He sanitized and bandaged Wiltz while Colonel Wade stared, gaining color. Santiago finished with the sergeant and took the colonel's pulse again, finding it slower and stronger.

"Why'd you do it, Wiltz?" demanded the colonel suddenly.

"Do what? Oh, that was an accident. Got a little wild."

"You tried for Toole, too, until he shot your hand."

"No accident, Colonel," said Santiago wearily. The day had scarcely begun, and he felt exhausted. "He had reasons. With Sapp and that Cottonmouth dead or dying, he had good reasons. He thought to walk away from this. Who'd know anything? You dead. Me dead. And Mimi too, I'm afraid.

Killed in the fusillade. Nothing but confused stories from the ladies and sports and teamsters.''

Colonel Wade reddened. ''Wiltz, it's the firing squad for you. I'm busting you to private.'' He stared. ''And you a sergeant major. Liggett dead. Four men now. You all tried to do something to help the army, I'll grant you that. A massacre that led to . . . to this. Your doing, Wiltz. I see you behind it all.''

Wiltz laughed roughly, until pain quieted him. That and the bore of Mimi's revolver, pointed steadily at his forehead.

''Give me an excuse,'' she said.

Santiago recruited teamsters to carry Wiltz, Colonel Wade, and the body of Liggett to Keogh and the infirmary.

He manacled Wiltz, just in case. ''Bring the hand-irons back to me, and I'll want statements from you as soon as possible,'' he said. ''They'll no doubt send officers and men back with you.''

He took brief statements from the rest, writing until his fingers wearied. None had witnessed the shooting because they had hugged the floor behind cover. But they'd heard what went before, and that counted for much.

A swarm of blue-bloused men arrived about then, led by the adjutant, Lieutenant Jupiter Cortes. All in the teamsters' wagons. They'd already gotten the story.

''What do we do with them?'' Cortes asked, indicating the bodies.

''Bury them, I guess. I'll get that gold in Sapp's skull. Belongs to his heirs, or the county.''

''You worry about that?''

Toole smiled. ''I uphold the law. We'll advertise three times for heirs. After that, the county will probably acquire it.''

''I thought to burn the place.''

''It's not yours to burn, Lieutenant. It's well built. See the labor in it? There's lots of things it could be, including a guildhall or social center for those Norwegians. I'll hold the army responsible if anything happens here.''

''It'll become another Hogtown.''

''I think the county will heed the wishes of the command at the Fort, Lieutenant.''

The sports and slatterns heard it all glumly, and turned to pack up. Santiago watched them silently. He emptied Cottonmouth's pockets of one thousand, five hundred and thirty-seven dollars, all greenbacks. He collected Cottonmouth's weapons and gunbelt, Sapp's murderous walking stick and his pepperbox, which had been converted to cartridge ammunition, and piled them in the buggy where Mimi sat, quietly waiting.

"There should be words spoken for Sapp and that Cottonmouth," he muttered to Mimi.

"Even for them?"

"Who knows what's in the mind of God?"

He prowled the building one last time, and then settled into his buggy and headed home. The herringbone skies hid the sun, but he thought it was afternoon.

"You waited. You didn't draw your gun. You didn't shoot for a long time," she said.

"I miscalculated. They threatened each other, Wiltz and Liggett, Sapp and Cottonmouth. The shotguns against the revolvers and the wolf. I saw no reason to draw or even threaten them. As long as I couldn't stop it, I thought to let them finish what they'd already started. But Sapp and Wiltz both reasoned differently . . . and shot at me. Or tried to. I defended myself and have no regrets. If anything, I shortened the suffering of the dying, including that wolf. Mimi, how do you feel?"

"Are you expecting me to feel guilty? I don't. They almost beat you to death. Attacked me. I came to defend you, Santo, and I did. You don't like to kill, so somebody has to. A sheriff has to, sometimes. But you're a doctor."

"No man likes to kill, doctor or no doctor."

"I'm not so sure of that. Cottonmouth did. Wiltz did too, I think. My mother's brothers. They loved nothing better than a Sioux or Blackfeet scalp."

Santiago didn't respond. He'd wrestled a thousand times with his strange circumstance, being an instrument of death and life at the same time. This time he'd shot dying men and a dying wolf. He searched himself, finding nothing to fault himself with. He didn't know if he had showed courage, but he knew he hadn't been a coward. He'd upheld the law, he'd faced deadly men, he'd struggled in some small way for China Belle. He felt oddly small in this vast wild land, and yet larger than the young doctor who'd sailed by White Star steamer from Ireland.

Welcome to the untamed world
of the WILD WEST,
land of opportunity and desperadoes . . .
where the true price of
women and gold may be a man's life!

If you liked *Incident at Forth Keogh*,
look for more westerns from
The Ballantine Publishing Group . . .

HANGMAN'S LEGACY
by Frederic Bean

WOLF MOON
by Ed Gorman

OUTLAW'S JUSTICE
by A. J. Arnold

THE WETHERBYS
by G. Clifton Wisler

Published by The Ballantine Publishing Group.
Available at bookstores everywhere.

Don't miss this exciting western!

THREE RODE NORTH
by
Marvin Albert

Clayburn couldn't care less about politics south
of the border, but when hired-killer Dietrich
murdered the man who was like a father to him,
it was time for the gunfighting gambler
to get involved.

Trouble was, Dietrich was the right arm of
notorious General Otero, and they were both
holed up with a small army in the impenetrable
fortress in Losquadros Canyon. Once inside, the
only escape route was a deadly, uncharted
underground river. It's a good thing Clayburn
didn't mind long odds, because this time
to lose was to die.